Echo of the Desk

Flairs and Glairs
Publication House

"Echo of the Desk"

ISBN No: " 978-93-91302-68-9"
1st Edition
Language – English and Hindi

Flairs and Glairs
Publication House
Regd. Under MSME Act.

Disclaimer

This is a work of fiction and solely represent the thoughts of the corresponding authors of the articles. Our editors have tried their best to edit the content of all the authors and check the plagiarism.

All the write-ups in this book are unique and are only published in this book.

In case any plagiarism or error is found, only the author is responsible alone, and not the publisher or the Compilers.

Cover Designing and Book Formatting

Shubham Shah and Ishani Agarwal

Acknowledgement

The world is a better place thanks to people who want to develop and lead others. What makes "Echo of the Desk" even more special are the people who shared the gift of their time and talent with us. Thanks to everyone who strived to grow while creating such a beautiful anthology.

We want to thank our parents for being our inspiration and constant supporters.

Without the experiences and support from founder and co-founder, Mr. Shubham Shah and Ishani Aggarwal and team at Flairs and Glairs, this book would not exist. Last but not the least, we would like to thank God for guiding us.

Co-Authors

Shubham Shah (Founder Flairs and Glairs)
Ishani Agarwal (Co-Founder Flairs and Glairs)

1. Wilbur Arnold Clarke (Compiler)
2. Parul Thakur (Compiler)
3. Shraddha Thakur
4. Sana Joseph
5. Sunita Jamuda
6. Ankita Sarkar
7. Devanshu Kapoor
8. Anushka Thapa
9. Suparna Roy
10. Prabhat Kumar
11. Somya Upadhyay
12. Rimjhim Sinha
13. Manasvi Agarwal
14. Jason Dias
15. Taniya Khemchandani
16. Tulika Singh
17. Jesvita Princy Quadras
18. Shabeena Khatoon
19. Palak Talwar
20. Sakshi Garg Jadhav
21. Preeti Mawri
22. Arushi Agarwal

Shubham Shah

(Founder- Flairs and Glairs)

Shubham Shah, an entrepreneur at "Flairs & Glairs" a brand with dynamics in events organizing and cultural educational pan INDIA, is a 26yrs old guy who recently has entered the digital platform of imprinting emotions. He has initiated with his own open mic platform to help budding poets and aspiring writers under his brand named as "Teekhe Zasbaaat"

He is a commerce graduate from the Bhagalpur City of Bihar. He states Writing has impersonated him since childhood and he has now been writing for over a decade!

Cooking, on the other hand, is his passion! He also mentions, trying out new things just tickles him!

When asked sir, Why SPICY EMOTIONS?

He smiled and added, “agar jasbaat teekhe na ho toh wo jasbaat kahan” Spices are all that blends! So do his words!

As a chef, he presents to you his dish! Hot and freshly served! Taste it! Feel it! Enjoy it! You can also find his writing in the Book “Teekhe Zasbaaat” and 50+ Co-authored anthologies. With his passion to explore opportunities across Platforms, he is working with keen devotion and We wish him all the very best for his future ventures.

He is Featured in the International Magazine DeMode for his upcoming solo novel.

He is Approved by Ne8x for its Lit Fest, and is a Golden Star Awards 2020 Winner.

He is a India Book of Records Holder for his Anthology Satrang, and has the Grandmaster title by Asia Book of Records, for the same.

He has also been featured in Prabhat Khabar, Dainik Jagran, and a lot of other Newspapers in Bihar for his achievements.

He has been a proud co-author to

India Book Of Records (Title- Black)

World Book Of Records (Title -15 Wonders of Poetries)

India Book Of Records (Title - Aaina)

Vajra World Records Holder (Title - Gustakhi Maaf Hai)

High Range of Records Holder (Title - Gustakhi Maaf Hai)

Indian Book of Records

(Title - Road from Worst to Best)

Share your reviews on his

INSTAGRAM

@spicy_emotions
@shubham4shah

Or via email on

shubham2shah@gmail.com

To stay tuned to his work and opportunities follow his business Handles

INSTAGRAM FACEBOOK YOUTUBE

@flairsandglairs
@teekhezasbaaat

WEBSITE:

https://flairsandglairs.in/
https://flairsandglairs.com/

Ishani Agarwal

(Co-Founder- Flairs and Glairs)

Ishani Agarwal hails from the City of Joy, Kolkata.
She is the co-founder of her Community "Teekhe Zasbaaat" and Flairs and Glairs Publication.
Been a Compiler for 45+ Anthologies, she is in the process for more. Co-authored in 150+ Anthologies. She is a India Book of Records Holder, a Vajra World Records Holder, a High Range of Records Holder, an OMG Book of Records Holder, a Bravo Record holder, a Forever Star Book of World Records and an Indian Book of Records Holder.
Approved by Ne8x for its Lit Fest 2020, and Literary Icon 2020. Also a Golden Star Awards Winner 2020.
She has also been awarded with India Star Republic Award 2021, a part of She Awards by Awards Arc and Winner of Nari Samman 2021 by Literoma.

She is also selected as Best Achiever of the Year by AwardsArc and Most Challenging Compiler Award by Spectrum Awards.
She got her first solo Published,a solo Compilation consisting of first 750 contents of hers, titled "Hand That Burnt While Healing".

She has been featured by the National Magazine "Taree Zameen Par" with the title 'unstoppable'.
Also featured in the International Magazine DeMode for her upcoming solo novel, she is proud to write on social issues, and is happy with the love she is receiving.
Connect with her on Instagram: @Ishani_agarwal_quotes / @compilations_so_far

Wilbur Arnold Clarke

Wilbur Arnold Clarke an aspiring 20 years old poet/actor/sketch artist was born and brought up in Faridabad, Haryana. He is currently pursuing Journalism from Lingaya's Lalita Devi Institute of Management and Sciences, Chattarpur, New Delhi and working as a Production Executive at Harikrit Films. His first compilation was Heart's Fortitude launched on 17th February, 2021.

You can check out other poems by Wilbur on https://ehsaas06.blogspot.com/?m=1 and follow him on his Instagram handle (@w.arnoldclarke6700) for more work.
You can also mail him at wilbur.jmc@gmail.com

School's First Crush

I was a seven-year-old boy,
When I fell in love with a girl.
We were in the same class,
Separated by a single desk.

All I could get was a good view,
Of her beauty which I could gaze upon endlessly.
I wanted to tell her how I felt for her,
But couldn't muster the courage as my mom was a teacher in the same school.

We both grew a little older,
I was nine and she was to become.
Sitting on the last bench,
Finally told her how I felt for her.

But she didn't feel the same,
And distanced herself from me.
I made continuous efforts to make her realise,
Until she said that she never liked me.

Shattering my heart into a million pieces,
Constantly thinking about that rejection.
That was the moment,
My life completely changed.

Blocked on every social media platform,
As I had become a little stalker.
Not knowing why was I stalking her?
Maybe because I could digest that rejection.

Ever since that day,

I never felt the same about you.
I wanted to call you Mine,
But the harsh reality forbids me.

After leaving that school,
I left all your memories behind.
Hoping that sometime,
You'll know what I felt for you.

Backbenchers

There was, is and will always be,
A unique and discreet group.
Commonly known as the back benchers,
Who really lived school life.

Discussing about movies and games,
Gossiping about their crushes and girlfriends.
Taking the longest breaks,
With naps in between lectures.

Not panicky about the teachers scolding,
Joking and picking up random fights.
To swearing not to submit their homework,
Because of just one friend not completing it.

Always taking the longest time to settle,
But no one could match them at sports.
Not too good at academics,
But never bothered to stress about it.

They were real gems at heart,
Always there for their classmates in any problem.
Just say a word,
And all will be standing together against all the mess.

They filled the air with mischief,
Hiding it behind their innocent smiles.
But were great artists,
And drew masterpieces on the desks.

They flew planes when the bell rang,
Land missiles before the next teacher arrived.

Lie with panache and credence,
Once they got caught.

With a constant flow,
Catcalls and comments shouted in the class.
Completing all assignments together,
Then submitting all together.

A lot more helpful than the studious ones,
Always jovial and cheerful.
More at peace with themselves,
But silently mischievous.

Enjoying always in class,
Still learning the most in a fun way.
Not bookish at all,
Fun loving but still the successful one's in life.

The Bus Stop

Early in the morning I'd jump out of bed,
And get ready quickly.
Reach the bus stop before time,
Just to get a glimpse of her.

As usual the was never on time,
Like it wanted me to gaze at her beauty for hours.
Little did I know,
That one day she'd be mine.

Seeing her in the morning,
Made my day a paradise.
Lost in her thoughts the whole day,
Keeping a smile on my face.

Hoping to see her once again,
When the bus would drop us back.
Following the same routine,
Again, n again, every day.

Parul Thakur

Parul Thakur writes about the various emotions that you encounter and fail to explain. She is a 19 year old freelance content writer hailing from Delhi, India. Her educational background is in journalism and mass communication (Currently pursuing) from Noida. Apart from writing, she loves birds and cooking. You can also check out her write-ups on https://paperboat-16.blogspot.com/?m=1.

The Old Fort

Ever seen a girl who talks like a maniac when in love and quiet with others? The girl who slapped her boyfriend in front of the whole school? Well, that girl is me. I am that girl.

Hi. I am Bismita Roy. The girl next desk in your school. I stand five-feet, ten inches tall and looked like an average girl who never dreamt of having a boyfriend maybe cause of consciousness towards own looks. I have a whitish-complexion, slim, hairs and a high-ponytail dressed in a school uniform. I had just completed my 10th class back then, was going to have my first class as a high-school student. To be honest, it was just another morning. Life was awesome. New beginnings. New stream.

I entered the school premises.

He looked quite young for an 18-year old. More like a baby. He was wearing red T-shirt with black strips on the shoulder and black trousers with a pair of black sneakers. I got mesmerized the moment I saw him. An aura surrounded which I loved. His fragrance filed the air and drove me crazy. He has small brown-eyes, cute stubble (I teased him upon). He had long fingers gripping his bag. We meet and introduced ourselves. His small eyes, seemed like a portal to another world of love, hugs, kisses and a lot of emotional attachment.

I felt like saying, "Please find attached" straight-away to him.

My best friend accompanied him giving me chance to befriend him. We decided to meet after school at Delhi's Purana Quila.

We walked through the green gardens of Purana Quila. We chatted about the most random things we three could talk about. It was now around 6.30 in the evening, time to go back.

The moment I boarded metro back home, I started missing his presence. The only time I didn't miss my love at first sight Mr. Cruise, it was the time I stalked his public Instagram profile.

Next day, I sat in the class and waited for the school to get over so I could meet him again. The bell rang. I was ecstatic and nervous. The wait was long, painful and nerve-racking. He exited the metro gates and our eyes locked. As he walked and smiled shyly, as he looked at me, I had to remind myself of breathing. I wish I had learned few poetic lines to tell him how mesmerizing and breathtaking he looked. I might impress him but he knew what a Dumbo I was at flirting.

That day, we walked through the streets of Central Delhi. We talked as if we were known to each other for many years. We discussed our insecurities, talked of our hobbies, favorite food, most loved parent and what not on earth. He grabbed my hands while crossing the roads, I swear in that very moment I wished only one thing that he should never leave my hand.

We kept meeting, though we never talked about whether or not we liked each other, or what our exes would think, or whether we should date or not, I was cautious about anything I said to him, scared that I might put him off.

Our meetings turned into non-date meetings.

We met at an old movie hall in Chandni Chowk. We got two tickets in second last row for Marjaavaan. As lights dimmed, I instinctively leaned into him. I put my hand across his arm and he didn't brush it off. I wanted to stop the movie and ask him what our friendship meant to him. Was it more than friends, on a serious note. But I was scared to lose that moment. I wanted to make most of it. The questions could wait on for another time. The movie ended, and right before its tearful climax. I wanted to kiss him. But I didn't.

That day, we texted each other at night and to my surprise he also wanted to kiss me. He confronted on the chat.

"When we we're watching movie, you came close 2-3 times and even closed your eyes. Were you moving in for a kiss? Don't judge or misunderstand."

"I wanted but didn't wanted it to be for fun." I said.

"I would have never done that for fun."

"I can kiss you but I don't want it to be another accident. And what would be we after that." I said.

"Same is with me. Mostly its loss of friendship and during past months I've been mostly ignored even when I'm right in front."

"Do you want to kiss me?" I asked.

"Only if you want to and feel comfortable."
Next, we decided to go back to Purana Quila. This time we explored Purana Quila hand in hand. After a complete tour round the monument, we sat on the wall facing the zoo of Delhi.

A silence hung around us. He looked at me and I looked at him. I didn't know what to say. I had no idea what it meant or where it would lead us. I didn't know what I had in mind.

I leaned into him. His eyes never letting go of mine. His hands clutched my face tighter. Still centimeters away from his lips, my eyes closed as I could already sense the overwhelming pressure. Time froze as my lips touched his, the soft wetness of his soft, pink lips against mine felt divine. Our bodies and then soul met. I lost my self in the kiss, as my lips warmed up to him and I kissed him out of passion not the googled ways. I didn't know what I was doing. I had lost my senses. The kiss lasted for a lifetime. My heart was beating out of my chest. The wetness and passion reached every iota of the blood rushing through my body.

I opened and closed my eyes periodically, I fell harder for him. And every time, I saw him he gripped me tighter as if he would never let me go.

I used to wait for him now and the reason, I could meet him.

I noticed every time I complimented him he would curl up into a pink ball (sweet candy – gudiya k baal, I wish I could eat him) that embarrassed me and he would just give his smile. The naughty smile.

Well, he never stops flirting with me after such a long time. Every time, we had to depart. We shook hands. He would hug me tighter. To be honest, his smell lasted longer or his touch. I can't decide till date.

When he walks away from me to the opposite platform, it seems like the world has come to an abrupt end.

I called him as soon as I reached home. I was not desperate but I couldn't help calling him. I don't know when he became my habit.

The late night talks with him have become a routine now. We talk for hours, tucked inside our blankets, whispering into our phone, as if we were together, he and I, hiding from the world.

Every Year, Every Month, Every day, Every hour, Every Minute, Every Second – I am falling more deeper in love and rising high with his wings.

Shraddha Thakur

Shraddha Thakur is a 10-year-old girl, studying in fifth class at Greenway Modern School. She likes creating and editing videos, clicking selfies, painting and cooking. She is also good at narrating stories. She loves dogs.

My School in 2021

My class teacher looked different,
I had a new teacher.
My classroom changed,
It is now a 5.5 inches screen.
We all study together,
But we are away because of distance.
Things have changed,
We wear masks now.
I don’t ride my Papa’s scooter to school,
Nor my mom works to make lunch early in the morning.
Now I sit by myself in my room,
I miss my mam saying
“Behave properly, it’s not your home.”
Now my class has pin-drop silence,
Because ma’am puts us on mute.
I miss shouting and singing,
“Gooooodddd Moooorrrnnning Mam”
With my friends.

I hope these changes disappears
And life get backs to normal.
The time when I rushed to school,
Because I got late because of my sister.
The time I took money from mumma,
To have samosa from canteen amma.
I miss you School.
I will come back soon.

Class Monitor

Once upon a time, there was a girl – Akriti in Shiksha School. She was good at studies and sports. She played basketball. One day, her teacher called her out. She announced to the class as Akriti was good in studies and sports she will be the new monitor of the class.

Akriti was happy as she was now monitor but afraid because she never fulfilled the duties of monitor earlier.
“Mam, I don’t know how to become a monitor.”
“Why, beta?” said the teacher.

“Mam, I was never a class monitor before.”
“It’s okay. I will help you.” said the teacher.
From that day, Akriti used to sit on first bench. Teacher assigned her various task like make class list, collect notebooks, go to staff room, etc. Akriti was happy as she was enjoying her duty a lot.

But one day, teacher had to go to meet principal of school urgently. She called Akriti.

“Akriti, I am going to meet our principal. Please look after the class and maintain discipline.”
“Ok ma’am.”
Ma’am goes to meet the principal.

All students start playing and change their seats. Akriti tells them to stay quiet but they don’t listen to her. When ma’am comes, she scolds Akriti. This happens many time.

This time when teacher goes to library. She tells Akriti to write name of disturbing students on board and don’t say anything to anyone. She writes name and when ma'am comes back, she punishes those students.

After punishments, student decide to stop talking to Akriti. They believed she was the reason for their punishments.

Akriti feels lonely and tells her mom that she will now quit from monitor post. She was not happy being the monitor. Her mother asks her what happened because earlier she liked being the monitor.

Akriti tells everything to her mother. Her mother listens to her carefully. Then she whispers a trick into the ears of Akriti.

Now, next time when teacher went to meet someone. Akriti came to monitor but said something to everyone.

"Hello everyone. I really like being the monitor but I understand if I write your name you get punishment. So, from now if you talk slowly, I will not write your name and you will not get punishment.

Everyone Agreed.

Supermom

Thank you, Ma'am,
I don't what would be I without you.
You have always supported me,
Done things no one did.
You fed me more that
My stomach could take.
Thank you, Ma'am,
I don't what would be I without you.
You made me finish my dabba
In the break.
My mom was proud of me,
Coz I finished my food,
But you were behind this fame.
Thank you, Ma'am,
I don't what would be I without you.
Whenever I got a zero in test,
You scolded me in front of class,
But cheered me up in the end to perform better.
You helped me learn importance of time,
By telling me to reach school before time.
Thank you, Ma'am,
I don't what would be I without you.
When my parents became angry,
In the parents meet and ready to punish me,
You came to my rescue,
By ensuring better result next time.
Thank you, Ma'am,
I don't what would be I without you.
In this world,
No one cares for anyone,
But you care like my mom,
You comfort me like dad.

Thank you, Ma'am,
I don't what would be I without you.
I know you hold back tears,
When I hurt you.
But I love you ma'am and never stop loving you,
You will also never stop loving me I know.
You are a supermom ma'am.
Thank you, Ma'am,
I don't what would be I without you.

Sana Joseph

SJ is an eighth grader from Gurugram. She is an avid reader, ancient mythologies and fictions interests her the most. She also loves to do all sorts of art work and write anecdotes. Her past time also includes playing with her furry friend. She has been awarded multiple times for her amazing oratory skills. Her creative art work and her humbleness towards others makes her out shine.

THE PHANTOM ISLAND

It all started when my best friend blew up the chemistry lab. Okay, I should probably back up and tell you the whole thing.

My name is Estelle Miller. I'm thirteen years old. Until a few months ago, I was a student at Brearley School, a private school for girls on the Upper East Side neighborhood in the borough of Manhattan.

It was a normal morning, had breakfast and a goodbye hug from mom and a pat on the back from dad. Dad drops me to school before going to work but sometimes when he has to go early, I walk to school. It's just a 7-8 minutes' drive to school, but today we had to pick Alex too. I and Alex have been best friends since first grade. Our friendship started when a beefy girl named Kelly snatched my favorite lead pencil from my hand and I started crying. Alex just snatched the pencil from her hands and gave it to me; I wasn't sure who was more surprised me or Kelly. Her real name is Alexandra, but she insisted on being called Alex because she thinks it sounds cool. She has shoulder-length blonde hair, brown eyes and is half a head taller than me.
We waited for 15 minutes in front of Alex's house, and dad honked twice before she came out, half running-half hobbling and a half-eaten waffle in her mouth, holding her bag in one hand and in the other a sweat shirt. Her shoe laces were untied, she wore a black T-shirt with a broken-heart print and her favorite ripped jeans. Her blond hair tied in a high-ponytail. She looked up at me and my dad, she grinned, or well, at least tried to, said a muffled 'Morning Mr. Miller,' and sat in the back of the car.

They started talking about the usual stuff, parents and studies to which I didn't pay any attention. When we finally reached school, I took my bag and hopped off the car. Alex and I waved our goodbyes to Dad, and walked towards our homeroom.

I and Alex met in front of the cafeteria, for our third class of the day, Chemistry. The girls in our grade had silly excuse that doing the experiments in the Chemistry lab will ruin their manicures, even after wearing gloves. Except me and Alex, we totally love this class because firstly, the lab incharge, Ms. Kyle, a short heighted woman with purple highlights in her dark hair is a really sweet person and secondly, we both love when things explode. Like the last time when Alex and I dumped 45 packs of Mentos, in a large bucket filled with Coke. That was epic, but we both got grounded for a week after that.

Anyway, when we reached the lab, Ms. Kyle was arranging sand in a circular tray, the size of a truck's tire. We all filed in around it and she looked up and smiled, 'Hey guys, today we're going to have a fun day!', everybody around groaned and complained, and Alex smirked. Ms. Kyle stood up and dusted herself off. "Now, children. Believe me, it's going to be a fabulous experiment', her eyes sparkled with excitement.

'What, exactly, are we going to do?,' someone said from behind.

'Good question, my dear. We're going to make fire snakes!', she said. Alex and I looked at each other with wide eyes, she mouthed 'Awesome', and I nodded. I had to agree with her, after the Mentos-in-Coke experiment, we weren't allowed to do any exploding stuff, which is why I was really looking forward to do this. Ms. Kyle gave us some instructions, and divided us into three groups to mix the materials. There were

five of us in each of the three group. I was in a group with Alex, Bridget, a petite girl, and two other girls, whose names I didn't know.
Ms. Kyle made us put all the materials together. Then passed one of the lighter to me for burning the liquid fuel-absorbed-sand, seeing my stunned expression, she said 'Well, I need someone to help me. It's going to take a long time to burn.' We burned the sand and then waited for the fire snake to make its way out. I have seen many videos of this experiment on the internet, the snake is really just a black-irregular looking…. Snake.

We waited but nothing happened even after Ms. Kyle poked at the sand. The lighter was still in my hand so, I thought maybe it needs more fire and started to light it again.

That's when everything went wrong.

My hand was just a few inches away from the sand when, Alex yelled something I couldn't identify, a force pushed me, the lighter flew from my hand and my head hit the floor. My vision blurred, I heard the others shouting and running. I had no idea what was happening, pushing myself up in a sitting position, I saw something so weird, even weirder than my dreams and believe me I have the weirdest dreams that I almost fell back again.

Alex was sitting near the circle tray, which was on fire and somehow wasn't even touching her even though the fire was spreading throughout the room. Her eyes were closed in concentration, her mouth moving silently as if she were chanting but the strangest thing was the sparks that flew from her hands and joined the fire. The sparks were green in color. I couldn't remember anything that Alex must have told me, about her having superpowers. I tried to stay calm and yelled her name, but it was of no use. I looked around the room looking for something to throw really hard on her head. Now, I am a good friend but you have to take such measures when your friend goes crazy with fire. Near the doorway, I saw Bridget trying to help a girl whose leg was pinned under a table. I rushed to my feet to help them, we picked the table from one side and the girl's leg was freed.

'Go! Get out of here!' I told them. They nodded and ran out of the room, just in time before the door came crashing down, burning. Okay, I told myself, I'm not getting out that way.

I looked around to see if anybody else was left. Nobody, except me and Alex. I was extremely terrified and had even lesser time now, the fire was spreading fast. Then I found just the thing I needed. A broken chair leg, just the right weight not too heavy, not too light just right to knock Alex down. I picked it up and threw it towards Alex. I would like to tell you that it hit right on the head and I stopped the fire and saved the day.

But nooooooo.

That didn't happen. I never miss my target but today when it was needed, I missed. I looked around for something else to throw, the fire had surrounded me except from the front, where Alex was sitting. It singed the hair on my arms and made my eyes water. At the corner of my eye, something glinted. Oh, joy! It was Ms. Kyle's Golden locket. I picked it up, thinking if it'll work. I started swinging it round and round, faster and faster and then I let it go.

It hit Alex right in the middle of her forehead and she collapsed. I rushed forward and pulled her away from the fire tray. She was really heavy and her head was lolling backwards with her mouth open, which would have been funny if we

weren't in the middle of a burning room. The door was burning, and I backed towards the only wall which wasn't burning. It had windows. Our only way out, and the lab is on the first floor. It faces the school's courtyard. An idea started forming in my head, it was stupid and really, really risky but the only way. I took off the sweatshirt Alex was wearing over her T-shirt and tied it around us, in such a way that we were facing each other. It was a makeshift harness. I open the nearest window. It was wide enough for us, I climbed onto the pane which was hard with Alex tied to me. Without looking down I readied myself, took hold of Alex and jumped.
On our way down, I somehow got flipped and saw that I calculated wrong. The Chemistry lab was on the second floor. Oops, I thought, we're going to die now. Just as I thought this, a vortex of blinding white light opened up in mid-air. A hand reached out to us, and I did the most sensible thing, I grabbed it. The hand pulled us up. Then I blacked out.

When I gained consciousness again, it felt like I was sleeping on my bed in my house. The memories of the fire flashed before my eyes. I sat and my body racked with pain. Ignoring the pain, I looked around the room. The room was bare, except it had a small table fan on the floor, a full-length mirror next to a door, which I guessed would be the way out of the room, and the comfortable bed I was in. I was wearing the same clothes as before, though they were all clean. I looked at my hands, expecting soot covering them but they were clean. I got up to look at myself in the mirror. In the mirror, I saw myself as a girl with dark hair, which were singed a little, and green eyes. I was bare-footed and had angry red burns on my forearms and neck. I was wearing an olive T-shirt and jeans, which puzzled me because I was expecting to see some traces of the fire on them.

I couldn't find my sneakers, I opened the door and walked out. I found myself in a green meadow with a huge fountain. On the left were grooves of Palm and cedar trees and on the right was a flower garden, with all sorts of flowers. My mom could've named them all. Straight ahead, the grass changed to a pink sanded beach. The waves lapping against it, making a pleasant sound. Looking at the orange-yellow color of the sky I guessed it might be two or three in the afternoon.

It seemed exactly like the paradise which I used to imagine when I was small.

'Hello, dear. You're awake' someone behind me said, interrupting my train of thought.

I whirled around and saw a woman who looked like she was someone's grandmother. She had blue eyes, caramel-colored hair, which were spilling onto her shoulders from under a white scarf that she was wearing on her head with a white, mid-sleeved gown. Her smile was contagious. My cheeks were hurting from smiling back at her. I asked her, 'Who are you? What is this place? What am I doing here? And how long have I been asleep?'

'Shhh…. patience child. I am Aurelia, the guardian of Auxilium Paradisum. Gesturing around at the island with both her hands. She said the last two words with an accent that I didn't recognize.

'You and your friend needed help, so I summoned you here. It has only been three hours since you came here.' She continued.

THREE HOURS. I've been away from home in an unknown place for THREE HOURS. And I felt like curling into a ball, and cry.

‘Alex? Where’s she?’ I asked, feeling guilty that I hadn’t thought of her before.
‘She’s resting. Come, I’ll show you.’ She turned and walked towards the groove of trees. I had no choice so I followed her.

After walking for, what felt like, thirty minutes, we reached a lighted cave. Aurelia walked right in and I followed her. Inside the cave, there were light blue curtains dividing it into sections. On my left was a Lute, a musical instrument about which I had studied long ago. On my right was a curtain-covered section. There was a candle- lit chandelier hanging from the ceiling. Aurelia walked towards the section on my right that was curtained, and drew the curtains aside. There was a bed and a side table, in the section. On the bed was Alex. She was wearing the same clothes she was wearing, except that these too were clean like mine. Her eyes were closed, there was a huge welt on her forehead right where I hit her with the locket. I rushed to her side and checked her forehead. Her temperature was back to normal.

‘She’s just sleeping, Estelle. She’ll be alright. There was not much damage.’ Aurelia came to stand next to me.

‘Sleeping………wait, you know my name?’
‘You talk in your sleep.’ She smiled

‘I…yeah,’ blood rose to my cheeks, I have been told this so many times that I lost count.

‘Anyway, I think your friend, Alex, will be awake by the time my servants have prepared the dinner. Until, then you can tell me how that explosion was caused.’

My stomach growled, and I realized that I hadn't eaten anything since the explosion.
Aurelia raised an eyebrow, 'That was quite loud. I'll bring you a snack to eat while we talk.'
With that she disappeared behind another curtained-section and I looked at Alex, thinking what exactly had happened?

Aurelia and I were sitting outside the cave on a blanket. I was telling her about how, Alex caused the fire to erupt until the moment we were summoned by her. She was a good listener. I looked at her time to time, to see her reaction but she didn't show them. As for the snack, she brought me some roasted peanuts that tasted awesome.

When I finished telling her about the events that occurred and I waited for her response. She nodded 'Your friend was possessed by a rogue spirit. An evil spirit.'

'A rogue spirit? But why did it possess Alex? I mean there were a lot of us in that room.' There were so many questions swirling in my head, it felt as if I was drowning, not being able to hold anything to keep me anchored.

'The spirits who aren't able to reach the Great Beyond, get lost and turn evil trying to make themselves alive again.' She explained

'The Great Beyond......is it like the place where people go after death?'

'Yes, and as to why the spirit chose Alex, is because the spirit saw itself in her.'

'Whoa...wait, what do you mean the spirit saw itself in her?' I asked, mystified.

'When the spirit was alive, it must've shared some of its ambitions and nature, with Alex. So, it chose her.' She closed her eyes, deep in her thoughts.

I myself was so lost that I blurted out a meaningless question to Aurelia 'Who really are you? Other than being the guardian of the Island.'

She opened her eyes and smiled at me 'Estelle, I am a Magna Mater. Magna Mater means Great Mother. We are the protectors of the mortal world. We keep the lost spirits at bay.'

I recognized the word 'Magna', and I realized that all the words that I had heard Aurelia speak were in Latin. Then with a jolt, I wondered if that word that Alex yelled when she was possessed was in Latin too. Then I looked up, 'You said 'we'. You mean there are others like you?' I asked

'Yes. There are nine of us. The others at this time are in the other parts of the world. Each of us, having our own Islands.' She answered

'How come the humans never found your Islands?'

'The protectors aren't meant to be seen. These Islands exist everywhere and sometimes nowhere. These Islands are imaginary. They change as the new day begins.'

'But……I am seeing you right now.'

She smiled sadly 'Mortals do come sometimes. You are the first in this millennia though.'
My mouth fell open. Seeing my astonished expression, she said 'Child, I am an immortal. A millennia is a short period of time for us.'

I nodded, as if I understood and then asked the last question that was bothering me 'So that spirit that possessed Alex, Is it still out there?'

'No, dear. You destroyed the spirit. When Alex was unconscious, the spirit was forced to leave her body to keep the spell that made the fire grow, intact. I have to thank you for that.' She patted me on the shoulder.

I felt horrified, 'Thank you? Why are you thanking me for this? I killed a person.'

'Estelle, it wasn't a person. The spirit would only have caused chaos, if it hadn't been destroyed. You are a brave, girl.' She got up and dusted off her gown. 'Come. Let's check on your friend and eat dinner.' She walked into the cave.
I sat there for a moment, thinking about what had happened today and then got up and followed Aurelia inside.

I heard someone laughing and looked up. I saw Alex sitting on a table with Aurelia.

I ran to her and hugged her tightly. She hugged me back. When I stepped back, I looked at her. Her color had returned, her hair in a ponytail and her eyes sparkled as if she was going to do something mischievous. Then all of a sudden, I shouted, 'You, Alexandra Harris, are a very difficult friend.'

She laughed and all my anger drained out. It felt good to hear her laugh after a day full of unusual events. 'Yeah, thanks for getting that filthy spirit out of me.' I swatted on her arm, in a playful way.

'Okay children, sit down. Let's eat dinner.' Aurelia said. We sat down next to each other at the table and Aurelia clapped her hands twice. The food was laid down by five girls, who looked about my age and had silver-blonde hair, and white wings which made them look like Angels.

Alex's mouth fell open and when all the food was laid out, one of the girls reached out and closed her mouth. I burst out laughing and she glared at me. The servants went away and Aurelia started serving us the food. 'They are your servants?' I asked in awe. Aurelia nodded. There was chicken stew, a loaf of herb bread and a large jug of sparkling water. It may not sound very appetizing but that's because you haven't tasted it.

While eating, I filled up Alex on what had happened with Aurelia adding points here and there. After I finished, Alex was looking at me in wonder 'Except the part where you knocked me out. I didn't like that. Everything you did was super crazy. And you jumped us out of the window.... Wow just WOW!'

The girls with wings came and cleaned up everything. I was so full and sleepy that I couldn't even say no, when Aurelia asked if I wanted to eat some mint ice-cream. After Alex finished her ice-cream, we all went outside for a walk. The moon looked so beautiful, touching the tops of the trees. When we reached the beach, Aurelia sighed 'Well, I guess I have to tell you.'

'Tell us what?' Alex asked

'That whenever a mortal visits us, we have to replace their memories before they go back to the mortal world.' She met my eyes, and I was overwhelmed by the deep sadness in her blue eyes.

‘Hey, but these memories are the good ones!’ Alex complained.

‘I’m sorry but this is necessary. We used to send people without such replacements, but your kind has broken our promises, and spilled the secrets to the others. I cannot risk that again’ she said.

I did not want to lose these memories even though it started with a horrible event, I wanted to remember it. I wanted to remember Aurelia. I wanted to remember the food that we ate with her. Her Island that looked so much like the paradise I had imagined, when I was young. I wanted to remember this all as an adventure that I had with Alex.

Then I told Aurelia all of this, I told her that I wanted her to bind me and Alex in a promise, to keep today’s events with ourselves. As I said this all, I saw Alex and Aurelia were both looking at me with wide eyes. When I finished speaking, I looked at our host who looked quite stunned.

‘E, you…...you spoke in Latin. How…...?’ Alex’s voice trailed off.

‘What?’ I was puzzled

‘You spoke the Magna Verba, the Great Words. They are always spoken in Latin. You speak Latin very well.’ Aurelia said, smiling at me. It was a smile that a teacher gives to her pupil, when they master something.

‘I…uh, thank you.’ I smiled back at her.

‘Very well, I shall do as you have asked me to do. Are you two ready?’ She asked

‘What have you asked her to do? What do we need to ready for?’ Alex asked, looking at the two of us.

I forgot that Alex hadn’t understood anything that I had said, so I repeated it for her in English.

She nodded, And Aurelia started binding us in the promise. I understood each and every word she was saying.

‘Auxilium Vos recedemus a Te Deum: non enim loquetur a te hodie certe vidisti. Adiuro te dictum.’ Which meant ‘You will depart from the Auxilium Paradisum, speak not of the events seen by you today. I bind you to this promise.’

Alex and I looked at each other and I knew by her look that she had understood everything too.

I looked at Aurelia, and then hugged her, ‘Thank you’

She smiled, kissed me on my forehead and muttered some kind of blessing. She repeated this with Alex. ‘All the other people who you were with, will have their memories modified. Now, where do you want to go?’ she asked us

‘My house. Estelle, will be spending the night at my place.’ Alex said

I smiled

‘Okay then. Off you go.’ And with that Aurelia opened up the same vortex of blinding white light, by which she had brought us here.

‘It’s safe, just go through it and you’ll find yourself in Alex’s bedroom.’ She ensured us.

‘I’ll go first.’ Alex said

‘No, we’ll go together.’ I said, taking her hand.

We said our farewells to Aurelia and we jumped. The last memory I had of Aurelia, was when she smiled at us when we jumped.

We landed with a thump, in Alex’s room. The vortex was nowhere to be seen.

‘Well, that was an epic adventure.’ I told Alex, who was jumping on her bed.

She nodded, ‘I would name this adventure as ‘The Phantom Island.’

I smiled and sat next to her, ‘yeah, I like that. ‘The Phantom Island.’

Sunita Jamuda

Sunita Jamuda is from steel city Jamshedpur Jharkhand. She is a student of hotel management, aspiring to be a chef. In her meantime she loves to write and listen to music.

स्कूल की यादें।

छोटे- छोटे क़दमों से चल पहली बार उस आंगन में ,कदम रखा था।
घर के बाद पहली बार किसी दूसरे आंगन पर कदम रखा था।
मां ने ज़िक्र किया था इसका पर ले कर आज आयी थी।
शायद पहला दिन ऐसा ही रहता है,स्कूल (विद्यालय) का।

कितने नए दोस्त मिलते हैं,
लेकिन मां, को देख आंख नम रहती है।
सब एक दूसरे से एकदम अलग, फिर भी एक से होते हैं।
शिक्षक(टीचर्स) मां- पिता के बाद इनसे ही शिक्षा मिलती हैं।
उनसे भी अलग सा लगाव जुड़ जाता है।
उम्र के चौदह वर्ष यही बीत जाती हैं।
बचपन से लड़कपन तक का सफर यही पूरा होता है।
घर के बाद एक परिवार सा बन जाता है।
बहुत सी यादें बनती है यहां।
यारी के किस्से स्कूल की दीवारे होती है।
और स्कूल के मेज हमारी पढ़ाई की सारी खबर रखती हैं।

शिक्षक से भी कुछ ऐसा जुड़ाव हो जाता हैं,
उनसे मिली शिक्षा का असर मानो ज़िन्दगी भर रह जाता है, उनके साथ के पल भी भुलाए नहीं जाते।
और यारों की यारी उसकी तो क्या बात है।

कोई प्यार में मजनू बन जाता है ,तो कोई इसके नाम से दूर भागता है।
कोई क्लास(जमात) टॉपर ,
तो कुछ एवरेज (औसत),
कुछ शांत होते है तो कुछ अशांत।
फिर भी किस्से सबके अलग और खास होते हैं।

अपनी अपनी भविष्य की तैयारियां यहीं तो होती है।
लंच हाउर (दोपहर का भोजन) कई किस्से होते है।
लंच तो लंच हाउर के पहले ही खत्म हो जाता है।
स्कूल की गलियरो में भागना बेवजह।
दोस्तों के साथ स्कूल बंक कर घूमने जाने का भी अलग ही मज़ा था।
घर पर पढ़ने जाने के बहाने दोस्तों के साथ घूमना भी अलग आनंद देता था।
एक पानी की बोतल से पूरे क्लास(जमात) की प्यास भूजती थी,
कोई एक पानी की बोतल भरने जाए तो उसकी हाथ कम और पानी की बोतल ज़्यादा होते थे।

लाइब्रेरी में बैठ अपने भविष्य की तैयारी जोर से हुआ करती थीं।
मजाल है किसी की जो एक किताब भी उठा ले
फिर भी भविष्य की तैयारी जोरों से होती थी।
क्या करना है जीवन में या जीवन का क्या करना है,
इन सब के ख़्वाब यही बुनते है।
कभी सुबह उठ कर स्कूल ना जाने की इच्छा
और स्कूल के बाद बस एक बार स्कूल जाने की इच्छा।
स्कूल का ज़िक्र हो और गोलगप्पे और कैंटीन का ज़िक्र ना हो ऐसा बहुत कम होता है।
जेब में एक रुपया ना होना तो एक के गोलगप्पे से दस का खाना।
कैंटीन की सैंडविच बस एक मिनट में चट कर जाना।
लेक्चरर के वक़्त जोरो से नींद का आना,फिर भी आंखे खुली रखना।
समझ कुछ नहीं आता इसलिए एग्जाम (परीक्षा)से पहले सारी रात जाग दोस्त के साथ पढ़ाई कॉन्फ्रेंस (सम्मेलन)में करना।

फिर पीटीएम (PTM) का डर,
रिज़ल्ट का डर , रात की नींद उड़ा जाता है।

कितनी रातें जाग कर ,बातें होती थी।
सबके जन्मदिन मे े केक आ आना एक अलग सा लगता था।
शिक्षक दिवस पर नए कपड़े और फोन से फोटो खींचने की अलग ही अंदाज रहता था।

पहले दिन रोए थे घर से दूर जाने के डर से और आखिरी दिन रोए थे ,घर से फिर दुर जाने के एहसास से।

पहले दिन जो लोग अनजान थे, अब वो हमारी जान है, तब रोए थे तब जिन्हें नहीं जानते हैं यह सोच के आखिरी दिन रोए थे सबसे जान के अनजान ना बन जाने के डर से।

Ankita Sarkar

Ankita Sarkar is from Jamshedpur. She did her graduation on Hospitality Management and her specialization is on Food and Beverage Services... Currently she is pursuing Psychology on Child Development... She is not a professional writer but she expresses her emotions through words when she can't express verbally...

School Memories

Waking at up six but still always late,
Standing in front of a gate waiting for completing the prayer,
Sitting at the last bench and playing games,
Waiting for lunch break to have a share from my best friend,
Bunking classes and enjoying with friends,
Indeed, school was the best part of our lives.

Everyday same uniform with unadjustable tie,
Different kind of shoes with difficult task of finding socks,
Many sections with many classrooms,
One best friend with one favourite teacher,
Too many crushes with only one bench sharing partner,
One school but million memories.

Running in the big schoolyard,
During games period or lunch break,
Pushing each other while playing,
Making fun of each other when we fall while playing,
Fighting with each other who cheats in the game,
Crying for each other who gets hurt,
And then scolding from teachers for being disobedient.
Yes, these are school memories.

School is a place where we spend long hours,
Learning poems and stories of the world's legends,
About moral and social values,
The traditions and customs with equality,
Where we are trained with practical things for being practical in life.

School bag was heavy, but there was no stress,
Two pair of shoes and two pair of dress,

Waking up was difficult, dressing up was pain,
Classroom was circus and teachers called us rude,
Pencil was a knife and scale was a sword,
Oh school, you always make me smile.

School Days

Sitting on a last bench,
Anxiously waiting
For the bell to pass
Just a minute late
Teacher shuts the door
Being a diligent student
Is a tough task
What shall we do?
We always ask.
It started with a toddler
Getting dress and going on a campus
An appreciation from father, mother's back then;
The struggle of learning had just begun,
Got whipped, punished and bullied,
The journey of school was long but worth.
There were days which were boring but some were interesting,
It taught us not only about academics but morals as well,
This has shown me life is not static but dynamic.
Leaving us lot of memories to cherish.
Five little girls sitting on a bench
With eager to learn,
Scared from teachers but not from books,
Don't know whom to look,
Little thoughts are given to stray,
Anywhere so far away.

Devanshu Kapoor

Shayar hai woh kaayar nhi
Likhta hai sach woh liar nhi
Woh Dev hai
Sirf shabdon ka sewak!
Tera nhi!

The Desk
(safar school ka)

Beet tah waqt hai kitni jaldi,
Abhi toh aur shararte baki thi
karni thi aur galti
school ke gate se leke, school mate tak !
Kahani chalo dheere dheere sunata hu.

Baat “Pehli” ki hai,
Darre sehme shareef the
maa ki chunni ke bhaut kareeb thejana
nhi maa chord kar
woh school ke shaur ajeeb the,
Hitler si principal ghum ghum se the har pal.

Phir sama beet tah,
Baat hai dusri ki,
Baithenge toh chaddi buddy ke sath hiwoh
kisi aur se ladai kursi ki,
Garmiyo mei jaate jaate ghar woh mithi chuski kulfi ki,
zubaa'n pe woh thandak badi haseen thi.

Ab chalo thoda aage chalte hai.. Baat hai “Chatti” ki Thode shaitaan, thode shararti ho gae, homework kya tha hum befiqar ho gae!
Aur uss time jealousy toh kya hi thi hum toh bas “FLAMES” mei busy ho gae, gaaliyon ki fight nhi thitabh hum pen fight mei busy ho gae.

Chalo ab baat karte hai "Nauvi" ki, Nauka humari samjho paar hi ho gai kab hoshiyaar se nalayak ho gae pata hinhi chala, maa ka pyaar, ab baap ki lataadh ho gai!

Ab "Dasvi,Gyaarvi,Bahrvi" class bhaut pyaari, Hum out of control ho gae… out of the lot ho gae, Humein jo dikhe nhi woh teachers ki nazar mei Humein bhaut khot ho gae. Sara - Sara din ki hai bhaes.. todi-tudhvai bhaut haddiyan bhaut si desk sachi we created a mess. Dimaag na laga kabhi phir bhi nawabzade khelte the "Chess", school was heaven! par banate the kabhi kabhi hell! Chalo in the end jaisa bhi tha school Hum the whaa ke Raja woh tha humara Mahal.!

Sach mei kardu kya
end?nahi na..
Chalo phir aur suno..
Ab baat karta hu woh playground ki
woh games period ki, uss PT wale round ki..
aur woh happy-happy surrounding ki,
woh dushmani wali kahaniyan aapas ki, phir badli jo dosti mei kaii'n woh strong bonding ki.

Salaam hai ground tujhe salaam hai,
dil mei tere lie samm-maan hai
woh free periods ki tu aan-baan-shaan hai, tujh par gire, tujh par chale,tujh par bhage,tujh se lagwaai kaii'n cho'nte, tujhe maari laat,par tujhe buri na lagi koi baat woh backbenchers ka tu hi tha bhagwaan.

Ab baat karta hu subah-subah school aane ki, chotte the, rote the, darte the par jaise-jaise bade hue late comers mei shumaar hum hote the.
Phir late aane ke fine bhi bharte the
Principal ka office toh jaise thana tha
waha roz ke roz aana-jana tha,
aur salmaan bhai ka toh pata
nahipar gunda raaj humara tha.
School mei "Wanted" hum
bante the aise hum bande the.

Ab baat karta hu woh last period aur woh 15 minute pehle ki..
basta kandhe par, nigaah ek-ek lamhein par aur chalna woh safar par,
jo jata tha makhmali bistar ke gadde par aur sukoon bhari aankhon ki nind par,
lekin agar galti se boondein gire baarish ki toh yaad hai woh pani mei chhap-chhap pairo'n ki
woh har kadam par saath chalti hui mitti ki smell!
aur humara bag toh water proof hai
marte the khoob dail.

Ab baat karta hu
Exam ke dino ki,
jo puri na hui, unn nindo'n ki
woh raatein,woh kitaabein lagti bhayankar thi..
umeed humari bas ab Shiv Shankar se thi..

Jo padha dosto'n ke sath woh padhai saare saal se badh kar thi
aur dil mei ajeeb si dhak-dhak thi, jab woh safaed kagaz sajta tha maez par
toh hari om ka sajda zaroori tha.
Aur yun toh toppers hume khaas kuch pasand na the, par unn dino, unn se yaarana bas ek majboori tha.

Ab baat karta hu Exam Hall ki
woh gaano ki,aur jo kehte the bataenge sab kuch,phir na bta kar daga dene wale, unn shaano ki
aur jinse nazarein chaar hoti woh yaaro ki..
aata tujhe bhi kuch nahi, aata mujhe bhi kuch nahi aankhon-aankhon mei bas yahi baat hoti
ab paper ke baad bhookh gazab lagti
phir na tera khana na mera khana, paet mei hazam wahi hoti, jo bhi roti kisi ki haath lagti
Exam de kar nikal ne ke baad dil mei hoti thi, Ek hi duake na ho ab paper discussion pura nahi toh ho jaengehum bhasm,aur khatam ho jaega tashan pura.

Ab baat karta hu
Result Days ki..
Kisi ke ghar mei mithai, kisi ki ghar mei suttai ke lie chappal purchase ki
PTM par jate the report card lene toh sab baat karte the bas humare kamzor base ki, aur dostiya'n todne ki koshish ki jati, yeh keh kar ke "aapke bache ke dost tezz hai" phir parents bhi dil khol ke swagat karte the..
iss news fake ki.

har jagah shiqayat hi hoti thi
koi na baat karta tha school mei kie gae humare kaam naek ki.

Ab baat
karta hu
Style Statement
ki
Ghar ki galliyan narrow ho na ho, humari pent narrow zaroor hoti thi
Yeh teri bhabi hai, Apni crush par, woh nazarein jaise arrow hoti thi
Woh basement ki seediyan yaad hai jhaa'n aashiqui hoti thi..
Dil toota agr izhaar ka inqaar sunn kar toh ussi basement ki deeware humare aasuo'n ka sahara hoti thi.
Woh English teacher par ek dil fidaa zaroor tha phir gulaab de kar ek din ussi teacher se woh pitaa khoob tha aur nazara woh adhbhut tha.

Dev ko koi baat na hai bhuli
aaj bhi yaad hai,school mei kaha tha teacher ne ke tu hai aalsi bhaut, kuch soch..bas yahi kehna chahunga...
Tu aam bhaut hai, mujhe kaam bhaut
Mai aalsi, meri kalam furtili
Mere har “Ik” bol ka “Naam” aur “Daam” bhaut hai!.

Anushka Thapa

Anushka Thapa is a 19-year-old co-author from Delhi, India. She co-authored various experiences which we encountered. Her educational background is in journalism and mass communication (Currently pursuing) from Delhi. Apart from writing, she loves singing. Echo of the Desk is the first anthology where she is a co-author.

School Memories

Memory 1

This memory dates back when I was in class 10th. When the internals were the only thing which were coming on time. So, it was the time when boards were near. I used to be a good student but as soon as I hit puberty every sincerity went nowhere. Before 10th I will refer myself as a dumb nerd. Usually, front benchers use to talk about boards and students who have the guts to even say 'Boards', this word used to be scarier than our vice principal. I was also a front bencher but most of my friends were from the last bench and they all think that I study harder than anyone and I will surely get a high score in my internals and the truth is I don't study at all. Board exams were a month away and our internals started in the blink of an eye and the subject which I hated the most was maths.

I was in the examination hall having my worst day. I was blank when the question paper arrived and thrilled after reading questions. The questions were soldiers and the exam room was a battle field to me. I was fighting with soldiers with all my strength but when 10 marks questions started coming the soldiers turned into giants. Somehow, I managed to defeat all the soldiers and completed my paper with 2 extra supplementary. I was so much confident with my paper and looking me confident made other students unconfident. Even our class topper didn't take extra sheets.

On one terrible day...

It was the day when our marks were going to reveal . . .

I was so scared but I didn't show anyone. The whole classroom was scared as the teacher already said that 60% of class have to give re-exams. One thing about my maths teacher is that he doesn't calculate numbers after checking the paper. He picks out one student and makes him/her to calculate the whole paper. On that day I was the student whom he picked. I was scared because I know I am not going to pass the exam and he picked me to recheck and number the papers. I was in my class in the corner rechecking the papers. After 4-5 papers my answer sheet came into my hand, I looked into the sheet I was blank. I was failing the exam which means I have to give a re-exam. I was scared. I told the whole situation to my friend. She suggested filling the answers and told sir that he didn't check the answers. This idea blew my mind.

I stared at her for a while then I stared at my answer sheet and then I started writing correct answers in my sheet. After 1 hr I took the answer sheet and went to sir rapidly and asked him to recheck my paper. Sir was so busy that day he even didn't think about anything else. He just took my paper from my hands and started checking he gave me good grades.

I was failing that exam but my friend's idea came handy. I passed my internals by tricking my teacher. Well, I never guessed my teacher would be tricked so easily.

Anyways...

This whole scandal became my memory.

And I passed my Boards as well!

Memory 2

This story is a little scary one. This story is about my first encounter with a creepy thing. It was in grade 7th when summer vacations were still going on and our extra classes too. It really made us mad when we heard extra classes will be taken on summer vacation. After taking the class me and my 2 friends were still at the school as we were completing a group assignment. Well others had left the school already

only me and my two other friends were only who were present in the whole school. After completing the assignment, we decided to stay at school for a little time. In our school we have 4 floors with a terrace and we are not allowed to enter the terrace. I don’t know how stupid our mind can get we decided to check our terrace. I was scared and my other friend Meena too but in our trio, we had a one monster who was Naina, she doesn't care about anything or any situation until it is adventurous or thrilling. Somehow, she managed to make our mind.

After a few minutes we decided that we’ll just look at the terrace and come back as fast as we can. It was the deal in which we all agreed. We managed to pass the 4th floor without getting in cameras. Now we’re on the stairs of the terrace and we were a little bit scared too. We opened the gate and saw a beautiful scene. We saw our school ground from the top. It was a very pleasant moment for us but it didn’t last for long.

We saw something strange on the stairs. The gate was old so it was having a cracking old sound. The wind also started blowing at high speed. We saw that a strange black shadow was staring at us from behind the door. Meena was the first who noticed it then she told us someone is here. The whole moment got blanked in a moment. I could feel that all of us were stunned and when I myself saw that someone was there my hair on the back stood straight. I thought we would pass out at any moment in that situation. As I said earlier Naina doesn't care until it’s adventurous right? She was the one who stood up fearlessly and went to see what’s there. But Meera said she’ll go too and I was there looking dumbly at both and at the end I agreed too.

We slowly reached at the door and busted it in a flash but there was no one...

Then we decided to get back into our class, pack our things and get out of the school. When we went to our classroom,

we saw a kid was playing with our stuff. We got scared again, we thought that the kid is the ghost as there is no primary building in our school. How can a kid appear here and play with our stuff?

After a moment...

Our sweeper appeared and asked us why we didn't get back home. We explained to her that we were completing our assignment at the moment that kid came and said “Mummy” to that sweeper. Then we realise that the kid was our school’s sweeper child. We also assumed that the same child was there on the terrace staring at us. After that we never discussed this case and after that it blended in our memories. This was the creepiest memory that I ever faced in my life. We never again walked on the school terrace.

Suparna Roy

Suparna Roy is a Post-graduate student of English Literature from University of Kalyani. Right now, she is pursuing B.Ed. degree (teachers training course) from Central Modern college of Education. She has interest in the academic and research line to explore more 'deconstructive' ideas in the field of literature. She has gotten few of her works published too and is engaged in attending and presenting at workshops and seminars related to gender studies. She has done one month internship as Campus Ambassador for a Delhi based NGO- Hamari Pahchan, MANCH- National Speakers Assembly for three months, and also worked as a Research intern for one month under Think India Tribal Rights Forum. Right now, she is a Communicative English trainer at Inzpira, Kerela.

'Possibilities' of School Memories

Experience is large spectrum where individuality is an important branch of consideration. So, let's involve talking into possibilities a bit. What is the first concern that pings our mind when we hear the words- 'school memories'? How do we associate ourselves with the 'echoes' of the desks? Before I move to answer my experience, let's brainstorm a bit in an unconventional way of the numerous probable savoir-faire individuals can go through. Whenever we think of school days, we 'generally' associate them with the best part of our childhood, or to say it is only for the school days and everything centring around it that makes childhood dynamic, beautiful and palliative. General re-presentations of school life are very common. I have heard people saying, school life was the best because they made a lot of memories, remembering the scolding of teachers now feels soothing, the ringing of the school bell, the sharing of home-made tiffin, twenty hands jumping into one lunch-box, cleaning the board after the teacher leaves the classroom given sense of superiority, assisting the teacher with her work (oh I am teacher's favourite feelings!), waiting for the games period, hating or loving the Mathematics class, crush on a particular teacher and efforts to impress them, forgetting books and borrowing from the next section, participating in various competitions, planning where to go after the school ends, waiting for the final bell to ring; yet, feeling bad that the day ended soon and again waiting for the next day. These feelings are general, and generalizing is a tendency people suffer from. Everyone's school memory doesn't echo in the same way or reflects this general 'assumable' happiness! For some the desks are terror, for some classmates are horrible, for some teachers are an insult, for some the ringing of the last bell is a relief like coming to school the next day is a

punishment, for some tears are all that school gave! It is very important to consider all such possibilities that can exists when we decide to converse on the 'echoes', the 'memories' of a major part of everyone's life which can be a blessing, curse, or even both. There are people who would love to walk down the lane of school memories with laughter and jests along with other old school buddies after ten to fifteen years of their life, when they are settled down. Even some would hate to walk down the same path after ten to fifteen years of their lives in an evening when sitting with old buddies or may be just the new ones! All are not same; hence, individual experiences are not even the same. Expression and ability do so also get nurtured during this part of our childhood. School is in itself a world which can act both as a provender as well as oppressor to individual identities. I have seen few people loves to visit their school once they complete their high schooling, hence their memories of school life is a lot fun. While there are many who feels irksome even at the thought of crossing their school gate if it unfortunately falls on their way to work!

Keeping into consideration of all such possibilities, I would therefore like to share my personal/individual experience of childhood and what I really wish may change with time. So, when anyone asks me about my school life, in a word I prefer saying 'silhouette'; yet, it was also a 'niche'. Perplexing, right? But it is true. Although it did appear as a dark shade for me it was the place for which I learned to grow, learned to fight, and learned to survive. So, when I walk down this lane, trying to hear the 'echoes' the desk made, I remember a day in Lower Nursery, where the teacher helped to have my tiffin, another day in Upper Nursery when I cried because my place was taken and the very next day I hit that student. Then Upper KG, where the only memory I have was of my handkerchief. Moving onto classes one to four, the 'echoes' are ordinary. Our classes were divided into sections; I was in section A, from Lower Nursery till class ten. There was a group in our class, good in studies and in other activities. Talking about classes and studies, till class four I was an average student; hence, not many friends did I make! The teachers always preferred talking to them, asking them about what they love doing, they were so interactive. I also wished to become the same, so while I was in my third standard, during the social studies class, the teacher said that today's class will be about 'how we celebrate our birthdays?' I was not good in framing in sentences back then; however, I took the courage to expose my desire; although the teacher was only interested in few voices. Being an introvert, it was difficult, but I stood up and said how all my relatives are invited, my mother cooks my favourite dishes, etc. The teacher responded and maybe I'll remember this forever- "Learn to speak properly and then stand to speak", the entire class laughed at me. I sat down and wrote on my part of the desk that 'I was not good'. My desk mate tried to comfort me, but I silenced myself more after that. Participating in activities was not that difficult as teachers would make all participate and perform something. Things changed in the secondary sections. In class five I had a group, I was happy, that finally I have got friends. Performing any activity was then our choice. We choreographed a dance by ourselves and performed during the Teacher's day. We had our half- yearly exam after that, I did a terrible result in computer, and my parents were upset. But this was general; parents are upset on these issues. What perplexed me the most was, the group with whom I was friends started avoiding me from the next time, made excuses of not sitting with me in the class, we no longer ate tiffin together. I realized the reason because in the next computer class, the teacher insulted me in front of everyone. I never bothered them again; silence and isolation engulfed my school days, why- just because I was bad in

studies! In class six, a commute took place unexpectedly, the niche started growing, and the history teacher said “you are the most irritating girl in the class”, because I was not able to answer any questions she asked in the class. What’s the niche here? I scored the highest in History from the final exam in class six till ICSE. I eventually became extremely good in the humanities group, because I found study as an escape for me during those days, I had no friends, but all ‘classmates’ talked to me and yet made fun of me because I was good only in humanities subjects and failed in Mathematics, average in other science subjects. I was called ‘The lost Musketeer’ by the classmates, I was body-shamed, and I was called different names because I had curly hairs. I was not allowed to participate in group discussions by classmates, but my niche-humanities, assisted me in brawling with all these controversies. I never got support of any teacher, until I became a little good in studies. These may appear, or get judged as very trivial issues, but when minute things occur in majority, it becomes the only noticeable feature. My parents knew nothing about my daily struggle. But eventually I was okay to deal with them and operate them in my way. The ‘thirteen years’ of my secondary schooling bolstered in comprehending the meaning of both ‘silhouette’ and ‘niche’. During my farewell the only thing I missed was the desk where I sat, I drew many images there, wrote many things there, others cried, hugged each other, engaged into long conversations with teachers, and promised to take admission in the same school during higher secondary. I was happy, nothing remorseful occurred to me. I decided to get myself admit in a school far away and left the school with my result. My high schooling was beautiful! So, I only prefer saying these two years of my life whenever anyone asks how my school days were. But roots cannot be ignored especially when it helped me growing so much!

When I got admitted to a new school, I made amazing friends, participated in every occasion in my school, people appreciated my skills. Made startlingly pulchritudinous memories! Teachers scolded but also loved us a lot, lower grades were not discouraged or insulted, rather required and potential qualities of every student were appreciated. During school excursions, I had an amazing communication with teachers, my shattered confidence started growing again, I kept scoring highest in History and Economics, I was no longer body-shamed neither was I called names for having curly hair. Surprisingly, my friends, and classmates loved it and encouraged me to make various styles with it. I danced, I laughed, I enjoyed, I grew, and I studied too! I ranked third in humanities section during the ISC board exam and was even awarded scholarship. I cannot detail much about my high schooling, maybe because that was the most resplendent part of my life- those two years won the shady thirteen years of my life.

Today I often wonder what made both the schools so different, why were the teachers and students so mis mated, why that school lacked acceptance, possibilities and appreciation, why was 'groups' more demanding than unity in that school. The answers are yet to be looked for because these are the stories of many schools still now. But every child deserves to laugh and grow, but gets nothing like that. Thus, this was my version of the 'echoes', relatable or not, it's unknown but, maybe, there exists more spectrums of echoes that demands to be heard like- few enigmatic, few strenuous, few palliatives, and few laughable versions of the desks!!!

Prabhat Kumar

Prabhat Kumar is a dedicated writer from Sasaram, Bihar. He is doing Bachelor's in History from Veer Kunwar Singh University. Also, a UPSC Aspirant. He is a man full of emotions, dedicated to his works and had described his feelings and thoughts through his stories and poems. He likes to traveling, reading novels etc... He always wanted to write his book and this is his another Anthology and hope you are like his work!!!

स्कूल : खट्टी-मीठी यादें

गया तो था, किसी काम से उस गली में । अचानक एक हल्की सी यादों की झोंका मेरे बीते कल को छू गया। उन हवाओं ने मुझे खींच ले गई एक ऐसी जगह जहां बचपन के कुछ खास लम्हों ने मुझे धागों में बांध दिया। उस बड़ी इमारत जिसके दीवारों के रंग आज भी वैसे ही फीके पड़े थे पर उसके अंदर तो वो रंग थे जिसने हमारे सफेद पन्ने जैसे बचपन को रंगों से भर दिया था। उसकी वह बैल्कनी जिसकी दरार के गिरने की अनुमान मैं रोज लगाया करता था।

मेरी आँखों के सामने वह एक ऐसी इमारत थी जिसे एक झलक मे देख कर कोई स्कूल तो नहीं सोच सकता था। हाँ, शायद हमें भी इससे परे बड़ी-बड़ी महंगी स्कूल को देख लगता था। पर आज वह हमारे लिए तीर्थ से कम नहीं है, आखिर मैं हाथों में कलम लिए जो इन एक एक शब्दों को लिख रहा इसकी शुरुआत तो उस पेंसिल से बेंच पर रखें कॉपी पर 'क' लिखने के कशमकश से हुई।

मुझे याद हैं आज भी वह स्कूल का पहला दिन जब पापा हम दोनों भाई को स्कूल के क्लास तक लेकर आए। मेरे चेहरे पर बेचैनी और खुशी का अजीब संगम था। हाँ, मैं रोया नहीं पर मेरा छोटा भाई पापा के जाते ही बिलख कर रोने लगा था। पापा ने कैसे-कैसे डाँट कर उसको बैठा गए। मेरी निगाहे तो बस क्लासरूम में ही इधर-उधर घूम रही थी। इसी कमरे से मेरी ज्ञान पाने की यात्रा प्रारंभ होने वाली थी और साथ ही ज़िंदगी के किताब में नए अध्याय की शुरुआत थी।

मैं शुरू में काफी ज्यादा शर्मिला लड़का था और एक शांत बच्चा जो किसी से बहुत कम ही बात करता था, पर स्कूल मे कुछ ऐसे प्राणी मिलते है जिसके सामने आप अपने ज़िंदगी के हर पहलू को खुल कर सामने रखते हो, हाँ, आप सही सोच रहे है 'दोस्त"। यह सब वही लोग होते है जिसे आप अपना सारे रहस्य बताते है। दूसरी शब्द मे कहें तो दोस्त एक दूसरे के सेक्रेट्स के चलती फिरती किताब होते हैं। वो कहते है हर ग्रुप मे एक ऐसा दोस्त होता है जो काफी डरपोक और

कमजोर होता है और बाकी सब उसके रक्षक, डरपोक और कमजोर दिल का लड़का मेरे ग्रुप मे मैं ही एक था।

स्कूल मे हमारा ग्रुप बैकबेनचर था, पढ़ाई की दुनिया से थोड़ी दूरी था। पीछे बैठ कर बातें करना और कभी-कभी फ्यूचर प्लानिंग होता रहता था। मैं स्कूल में था तभी से कहानियाँ लिखने का शौक जग था और जब भी मैं कहानियाँ लिखता था तो हर दोस्त को उसमे रोल देता था, ऐसा लगता था जैसे फिल्म की कास्टिंग चल रही हो। क्लास के सबसे कोने में बैठ कर मैं सबको अपनी कहानियाँ सुनाया करता और सबकी दिमाग की सुई बस आगे के आने वाले सीन पर रहता। खैर इसका फल भी तो मिलता था, जब हम सब को सजा के तौर पर क्लास में खड़ा रहने का पनिश्मैंट दिया जाता। लंच टाइम में हर किसी के टिफ़िन में हर किसी का हिस्सा होता। रोहित को मैं तो आज भी नहीं भूल पाया उसका हिस्सा हर किसी के टिफ़िन में हुआ करता था। अविनाश जिसने मुझे जाने अनजाने काफी कुछ सिखाया, अगर किसी से स्कूल में सबसे ज्यादा झगड़ा भी हुआ तो अविनाश से ही, मेरे स्कूल का वो दोस्त जिसने मुझे काफी कुछ सिखाया। रोहित, शिवम, हिमांशु, सुशांत, विभूति कुछ ऐसा ही ग्रुप था हमसब का।

मैं आम तौर पर जिस भी क्लास में गया मुझे और मेरे ग्रुप को उसके सेक्शन बी में ही रखा जाता था और ऐसा मानते थे की सेक्शन ए में पढ़ने वाले बच्चे बैठते है और उनसे कमजोर सेक्शन B बैठते थे। कभी कभी तो समझ नहीं आता था हम जिस क्लास में होते है वो क्लास स्कूल का सबसे बदनाम क्लास होता था या हम ही बदनाम क्लास में ही जाते थे, टीचर और प्रिन्सपल सर के मुह से एक ही शब्द निकलता था – "यह क्लास रूम सबसे उदण्ड बच्चों से भरा हुआ हैं" अक्सर मैं स्कूल से जाता तो सोचता की बस होमवर्क ही तो हैं कर लेंगे घर जाकर, लेकिन पता न कैसे वो होमवर्क क्लासरूम मे आकर पूरा होता था, नहीं तो फ़िर सर या मैम की वो छड़ी जो हाथों पर पड़ता था.......... बस अब तो वह छड़ी भी याद आने लगी हैं। हम सब हर साल 26 जनवरी और 15 अगस्त का इंतेजार बस 2 चीजों के लिए करते थे विभूति के गानों और मिठाइयों का, सोचता इस साल कुछ

नया आया होगा पॉकेट में पर हर साल तो हमारे लिए सोनपापड़ी और लड्डू खास मेहमान थे।
क्लास के छूटी हो और साथ ही बारिश सुरू हो जाए तो मानो मन में खुशी के फ़वारे उठने लगते थे, घर तक जाना मेरे लिए एक रोमांच होता था, बारिश में भीगते बचते जाना। कंप्युटर लैब का तो बेशबारी से इंतजार होता था, इसलिए नहीं की एमएस ऑफिस सीखना हैं, इसलिए की गेम खेलना है और वो KBC वाला पैसे की जीत की खुशी का अलग ही एहसास था।
क्लास में खड़े होकर बुक्स पढ़ना और ब्लैक बोर्ड पर पूरे क्लास के सामने नहीं आने वालें सवाल के जवाब लिखना, दो ऐसे अवसर जिसका इंतज़ार मैं कभी नहीं करता था, मुझे लगता था इसके बदले मुझे बॉर्डर पर भेज दो पर ब्लैक बोर्ड पर न भेजो। मैं डरपोक था। इसलिए मैं लड़ाई झगड़े से दूर ही रहता, पर स्कूल में मेरे साथ कुछ ऐसा हुआ जो मेरे यादों में सामील हो गया और जिसमे मैंने पहली बार किसी पर अपना खतरनाक वाला गुस्सा दिखाया था। क्योंकि मैंने उसे गुस्से मैं एक मुक्का उसके सिने पर पूरे ताकत से दे मारा और मेरा विक्टिम कहीं दूर जाकर गिरा, थोड़ा फिल्मी हैं, पर वह स्कूल ही था, जहां मैंने पहली दफ़ा अपनी ज़िंदगी में किसी को मारा था।
स्कूल से काफी सारी ऐसी ही कितनी खूबसूरत पहलू और कहानियाँ जुड़ी हुई हैं। यह वही स्थान है जहां हमने काफी सारी गलतियाँ की और काफी सारी सिख भी लिया। आज भी जब स्कूल से गुजरता हूँ तो आँखों के सामने वो सारे तस्वीर छपने लगती हैं और दिलों में एक ही ख्याल आता है काश की वक़्त वही रुक जाता। मैं बचपन में जब भी स्कूल जाता था तो रास्ते में एक बड़ा और महंगा स्कूल पड़ता था तो मैं सोचता था की मेरा स्कूल कितना छोटा हैं और इतना बड़ा खेलने का प्लैग्राउड भी नहीं हैं, पर आज लगता है फरक नहीं पड़ता है की स्कूल कितना बड़ा है या कितना महंगा है, फ़र्क तो बस उस इमारत के कोने-कोने में छिपे छोटी से छोटी यादों से पड़ता हैं।
हाँ, धीरे-धीरे वक़्त बदल जाएगा और हम भी जिम्मेदारियों में बंध जाएंगे, नहीं मिलेगी वह स्पेशल टिफ़िन और नहीं मिलेगी क्लास के

के लैस बेंच का कोना जगह जिसके लिए शायद कितनी युद्ध हो चुके थे। वक़्त और किस्मत की मेहरबानी की हम सब एक दिन एक ऐसे मुकाम पर पहुँच जाएंगे की हमारे पास एक अच्छा रहने का जगह हो जाएगा या फ़िर एक अच्छा का महंगा और आलीशान घर मिल जाएगा, लेकिन क्लासरूम की वो बेंच की छोटी सी जगह जितनी खुशी और कहीं नहीं मिलेगी।

कभी गुज़र कर देखो उस गली से ....

Somya Upadhyay

Somya Upadhyay is a school student and she is new in this poetic world. According to her, she loves to express her feelings in words. She is from Bareilly a small city in U.P but her dreams are higher than the sky. Her dream is to become a doctor. She believes that every word has a temperature.

I WANT TO GO BACK

I used to hate all,
From my open hairs to a tied braid,
My school from Monday to Saturday a week,
From chasing my dreams to studying maths,
From my nerdy glasses and heavy bags.
But
Preparing for competitions was fun,
Since our periods were bunked.
Waking up was hard, getting ready was pain,
The best part was the holiday due to the rain.
Pencils and scales was our swords,
The gossips we did when we used to get bored,
Now I am missing the fun,
I am having no more.
School you were not that bad, you made me smile,
I want to go back just for a while.

मैं हारी कहां अभी

जब मेरे स्कूल के एक टेस्ट में कम नंबर आए तब मैं हार गई थी| मैं काफी दिनों तक रोई यह सोचकर इतने कम नंबर कैसे आए, पर मां के समझाने से समझ आया की एक छोटी सी परीक्षा मेरे आगे के भविष्य को बदल नहीं सकती| यह कविता लिखते समय मैंने खुद को और मेहनत करने को उत्सुक किया मैं हारी कहां अभी|

मैं उठाऊंगी,
गिरकर फिर संभल लूंगी|
हार मानना कहां आता है मुझे,
मैं तो जीत के ही दम लूंगी|
माना रोई थी मैं छिपकर,
पर हंसकर जहां को दिखाऊंगी|
मैं हारी कहां अभी,
जीत क्या है अब यह बताऊंगी|

हार नहीं थी वह तो सीख थी मेरी,
मुझे गिरकर संभलना सिखा गई|
मेहनत क्या है,
बताया उसने,
और हार भी तो जरूरी है,
यह सिखाया उसने|

MY SECOND HOME

When I first entered with my little steps
Quiet sobs and lost eyes.
Wondering am I safe,
The teachers were nice,
and a few friends I made,
It was different for me,
But I loved that space.
When the time passed it became familiar to me,
The school was now a fun zone,
Never thought that school will become my second home.

FINDING MYSELF....

When you are a teenager, you think differently, what matters to you are your school friends and recess to enjoy. Your obsession with a video game or your favorite songs, dream to become an astronaut or a singer. But when you come to higher classes, you have to choose your way and find yourself.

I am lost in my world,
I am lost in my dreams.
My eyes are dull,
In order to find the glitter.
My feet are halt,
To find the right way.

Landed in a dilemma,
To choose my way,
First will teach me to live.
The second will teach me to survive.

But in the journey to find gold,
I'm still lost in finding my Rainbow
To colour my life with his beautiful colours....

The world changed or I

I was a child,
Unknown to this world.
The school was annoying,
Every classmate was a friend,
Flowers used to attract me,
Smiles cheered me up,
Everyone seemed good,
Everything was beautiful,
Even strangers were nice.

But now when I am an adult,
Known to this world,
School is the best memory,
Even best friends are now Strangers.
Only thorns are there in the plants.
Smiles changed into dangerous smirks.
Everyone looks suspicious,
Everything is dark,
Even familiar ones are now wicked.

The world changed or
I was wrong when I was a child?

Rimjhim Sinha

Political Activist | MA in Sociology

Rimjhim identifies as a woman with minimum expectations and crazy presence of optimism, who tends to find happiness in the most unexpected and littlest incidents of her life. She regards Sociology as her life guru, finds conversations to be the only way to realise how similar we all are to each other, and believes that happiness is recognisable if one looks for it and has the patience to see its wings unfold gradually.

You Taught Me What I'm Made Of

"Life isn't a matter of milestones, but of moments."

-Rose Kennedy

Our schools play an integral part in determining who we become as a person, and memories shape our vision towards the world. Every school brings forth different kinds of learning and motivation, building and nourishing us as the human beings we grow up to be. At this time of my life, when I'm done with my university degree and am almost on the brink of becoming an earning contributor to the society, I have realised that I'm one of the lucky ones who can boast about a cherished school life. All the schools that I've been to have been active aiders of important life lessons, lessons that have helped me modify my life to run on the right path. The path that recognises my needs and strives to achieve them, but never thinks of diminishing someone else's happiness while executing the process. This essay will try to explore some of those milestones that turned out into moments of learning and made me who I am today.

The primary school that my parents had admitted me to, was apparently the most renowned one in the locality. We had just shifted to Kolkata and I was beginning to adjust myself with the children living within the government quarters. The most memorable experience from this school is from a reciting competition. This was my life's first competition and my entire family was immensely excited about my performance. My father and I had been practising since weeks and we were determined to ace it out. But right on the D-Day, my stomach gave up on me and all the energy and excitement was about to run down those pipes very soon. Was all my effort to learn the lines by heart supposed to be discarded only because I couldn't muster the strength to stand up? I'm sure my intestines had uttered an 'yes' but my brain hadn't agreed. After the umpteenth time of coming out of the loo, I looked at my mom

and said, “Take me to school. I will perform.” She was taken aback and she immediately looked towards my father. I don’t exactly remember how he might have reacted but I’m sure it did not end in a ‘no’ because within half an hour, we had already started walking towards my school. I was pretty late and it would have been wrong to keep my name enlisted when we could finally enter the gates and walked down the hall. The competition was just about to end as the last participant was getting ready to arrive on stage. My mother explained the entire scenario to the teacher and ended with the last wish that I had expressed while at home. That was enough to convince her and she immediately agreed to let me perform. I happened to impress all the judges and won the first prize for that competition! This was one of the first incidents that led me to understand the most prominent quality in myself – a very strong sense of willpower.

Moving up my life’s ladder, I changed my school to start my secondary segment of education. Now, this school was a comparatively bigger affair, and had a lot of amazing things scheduled for its students. Not only did it have talented and sensitive teachers but also events that took away the ‘boredom’ of school life. Waking up at 5AM to board the school bus never seemed like a hassle because we travelled towards a world of beloved experiences.

This school believed in encouraging extra-curricular talents to ensure wholesome development of its students as responsible human beings. The administration and the teachers believed that a child deserves to explore the various arenas of possibilities to recognise their calling – and this led to the most awaited festive celebration of all – Students’ Festival. This festival was one of its kind, and it included every possible element that a human might have to do in their lives. Starting from cleaning up your own classroom (yes, with brooms and mops, literally) and decorating it as neatly as possible to performing self-directed plays at the make-shift stage built for

this celebration – it had all. To become a part, one had to be at least a student of Class 6, so for the first 5 years, all the students waited in anticipation of amazement. Considering my participation from Class 6, I was mainly involved in the cleaning and decorating work, because I did not have any clue about my cultural side. The cultural showdown was the last event in the series that generally decided who would become the winner of Students' Festival and hold the trophy for significantly an entire year.

So, the incident I'm about to disclose happened when I was a student of Class 12, and it was time to gear up for the upcoming Students' Festival. I did not want to limit myself to cleaning and had been looking for relevant openings in the cultural activities, so that I could fit in somehow, anywhere. I felt like I can do anything. I could sing, dance, act, do a magic show maybe (you know, the feeling you get when you desperately want to change your current job)! Luckily, I had one of my close friends as the in-charge of the cultural section, who had been deciding whom to fit where. I grabbed the chance to claim a role in the drama that was awaiting its rehearsals. I auditioned and got finalised for the role of the main character's sister, and the series of rehearsals begun. On our final performance day, our nervousness was almost about to reach its peak. Being the representatives of the senior-most class, getting defeated would mean a year of cat-calling by juniors – a horrendous experience (we were adolescents, it meant too much)! Class 12 was scheduled to perform last, and once we were done with our drama, the entire judges panel went silent. All we could hear was muffled laughter from the students of Class 11, who almost believed that the tradition will be sustained – Class 11 had always been the winner of Students' Festival since the beginning of it, Class 12 had never been able to score a goal.

A few moments later, our principal stood up and looked towards our team of performers. She called up one of our Life

Science teachers and had a 2-minute discreet conversation with him. Right after that, our teacher took up the mike to announce and I quote, "Class 12 has exhibited a stupendous performance today and we are extremely proud to hand over the SF Trophy to them this year!" – our entire class, including the spectators standing on the 3rd floor, started running down the stairs to congratulate and celebrate this historical change – "I also want to add, that according to our principal decision, this drama unchanged, is going to represent our school in the dramatic exhibition organised by NSD (National School of Drama) coming soon in the month of October, next year."

This, was enough to bring out the tears which we had been resisting with all our might. Not only did we win the festival, but we, our self-directed play, got nominated to represent our school in the drama exhibition of the most renowned drama school, NSD! This incident taught me, that essentially with hard work and patience, one can achieve goals that are otherwise regarded as impossible according to 'history'. All one needs to do is hold on, and believe in the efforts put in towards goal attainment.

It is practically impossible to elaborate on each of the incidents that shaped my career throughout my school life, but I believe it would be wrong if I didn't include the sheer joy of achieving the 'Best Play' title from none other than National School of Drama next year, which made all of us realise how strongly potent we all were and how significantly motivating can the idea of team spirit turn out to be.

It would be wrong to not include how in Class 11, I had played as the Vice-Captain of the winning team and got nominated as the captain of the same team next year, which could only go up to becoming the runner's up of the tournament. This taught me how being humble and accepting failures can create a more patient self which can steadily develop its wings to fly higher while facing further hurdles. This taught me how important it

was to enjoy the game, rather than to win it, and how satisfying it is to even fail with the team that loves to be regarded as one. Schools occupy the longest segment of one's career and therefore play a very significant role in determining the mental development and well-being of an individual. It is only when one tends to have a healthy school life, is when they tend to make better decisions in life. It is important for schools to understand the responsibility of developing a child's mind holistically and ensuring the safest environment for a child's exploring capabilities. Increase in cherished school memories would entail an increase in happy individuals aiding subsequently in the construction of a happier society. Once we understand the relevance and reliability of this cycle, we can easily fulfil our latent wish of experiencing a better society.

Manasvi Agarwal

A passionate writer, hustler, learner!
Manasvi Agarwal is a pre-final B. Tech student. She is a keen listener, active, creative, and technology enthusiast. Pen and Paper have always been her go-to-buddies. It all started as a rambling of words on the diary. She believes that writing sets her soul on fire and keeps her calm. Apart from writing she likes to read, dance, and explore new places and things. She is kind of an adventurous person. She is a storyteller by heart and writer by work. You can connect with her on Email: manasviagarwal4@gmail.com

Down memory Lane

We start our school life at a very stage. Before we can understand its importance, and before we see what is really in it for us.
The day most horrendous; the first day of school is one that still makes grown men and women cringe when they think back in time. You walk inside a strange big building, holding the hands of your parents. You grip onto your parent's shirts in tears as they begin to leave. The window fogs up with your every breath while staring them go through that door. You cry, wondering if you will ever again see those people who you love the most.
I remember way back during my school days, I used to hate waking up in the morning (which I still do) and dress up to go to school, reminiscing all the previous day's work that was forced upon us all. I used to think within every day, "Damn! When will I grow up and end up releasing all the burden and pressure of studies"? But now I would just do anything to go back to my school days, sit in my classroom, play red hands and various other outdoor games with my friends, exchange intriguing gossip on who has a crush on whom. I bet there are a zillion other memories that we have about our childhood school days, what about rejuvenating them right here, right now?

Another year older and wiser!

My friends used to wear casuals on their birthday, the entire class sings 'Happy Birthday to You', distributing chocolates and then taking your BFF along with you to give chocolates to the teachers in the entire school. Undoubtedly, we all want to relive this memory.

Unfortunately, I never wore casuals nor distributed chocolates idk why. I was like " chal na kaun kr rha" always. Though I loved joining my friends for distributing toffees as it was kinda official chance to bunk classes.

Adrenaline Rush!

I never skipped any classes but when our subject teacher was absent, I always wished "Arun Sir" to arrive as a substitute teacher. He was the crush of all the girls. Yaayyyy! The free period was the best thing ever, only when the substitute teacher sets you free to do anything.

Booom!

Diwali was the best time ever to go to school coz we got to sneakily explode bombs in the loo or ground. We were like pros in doing it coz I don't remember getting caught even once. I was the one who keeps a check on teachers. Wish I still had such amazing talents to do stuff so sneakily.

Fever of joy!

School time would be incomplete without these huge celebrations. I still remember how much excitement we had of wearing a saree for the first time in school. Flag hoisting and march past on independence and republic day, dance performances and games on teachers and labors day are major nostalgic. The extreme joy was during school elections. I was the reporter and handling the whole media team. While writing also I am laughing very hard.

"Good morning, Welcome to KDB Public school, so how excited you all are to know who will be the winner" "Let's wait for some time till then keep voting .... I am Manasvi with cameraman bla bla" . Lmao, I am unable to recall who was the cameraman. But that day was one of the best memories I have.

Gamesss!

A happy morning face when we realize it's that day of the week. As long as we got to play, we just won't care whether summers, winters or monsoons. With all our energy we were ready to play outdoors.

PT (Physical Training) sucked a lot. I can't express that anger when it's your game period and the teacher be like "Aj koi game Nhi only PT" I was like what's wrong with you man "Ek period milta h usme b ye PT pure time mtlb kuch bhi"

Love cum Fun!

Hahaha! Valentine's week used to be epic. Remember when guys decide to celebrate each day just to impress a girl. Ufff! So funny damn. Gifting teddy, rose and chocolates just to impress the crush.

"Kya hua maangyi" "Nhi yaar" that pale face of boys still fills me with laughter.

Lunch m kya layi hai?

My day began with Lunch m kya laye ho sb? I always ate lunch before recess. Though every student did this once in their school time. If not mine, me and my friends would steal someone else's lunchbox and gobble all of it down and pretend as if we are listening to the teacher very carefully by nodding and making serious facial expressions.

House Dress :|

There always used to be this one person who would forget to wear whites on Wednesdays and that was none other but me. I didn't like my house t-shirt color (yellow). I was so mad that I'm always ready to get punishment but will never wear that t-shirt.

"Chair bnjao sb 15 min k liye" "jab drd honge per tab agli bar se aaoge proper uniform m"

But I was so stubborn I always opt punishment.

Throughout the years, our achievement alters as does the effort that we put. Our goals keep on changing so our friends. It becomes much clearer that we can try something with whole determination and perseverance and not succeed but it helps us see the difference between the things that aren't meant for our future and the things that we relish and could spend the rest of our life doing. The time comes when the end is nigh and it feels as if we cannot do anything now, feels like everything seems to get blurred. Then we nudge ourselves that there is nothing left to go, but we might as well complete it to the best of our abilities, like a sprint at the end of a prolonged race.

In the end, we look back, see our achievements, lessons learned, and the purpose of this place we call the school. It seems as if our lives can stay uncomplicated, but the main goal is to grow up and walk in opposite ways. We appraise what we have learned and the opportunities created for us. But when the big wide world opens up for us, only then we value our school days.; where we learn and enjoy the events that school life brings to us. We could continue our lives the same way it used to be only when we come across the true side of life.

Jason Dias

Jason Dias, an avid writer of short stories and poems hails from Goa. His interest in writing developed during his college years. He attributes his success in writing to his Mom, few of his cousins, Zamila, Andrea, Aarya, Bazilio, Ishana, Edna, Syona, Marushka, Clifford and a couple of others friends who believed in him and supported him throughout. He is passionate about playing football, basketball, singing, strumming the guitar, writing songs and acting.

A GLIMPSE OF FOND MEMORIES

Schools are the places where we meet friends and create the best memories of our life. My school journey included the best years of my life. Let me take you guys to few of those days which will never fade away.

On 5 June 2011, I joined Class 5th of St. Britto's high school, Mapusa- Goa with joy along with an addition of some new amazing friends. It was an all-boys school. The school area was very large with a priest's residence attached to it. There were 2 basketball courts, a large football ground, a pull up bar and a ground in front of the stage which till today I'm still figuring out what it was actually used for. Every class had 3 divisions namely A, B and C. To be honest, I was the crankiest student in the school. So, if any teacher scolded me, I would cry and yes, the whole class used to laugh. The best lecture was Physical Education (P.E) because we were allowed to play. I'm sure everyone reading this will agree that the worst part of school is when your P.E teacher is absent and the maths teacher comes and completes her class instead of letting us out. I had a few friends which changed during the years because of the divisions. I was that guy in the class who never completed his books. The worst memory of Class 5 was during an exam where I completed only one side of the paper and sat calmly for an hour as in my previous school, we were always given a single sided paper. Later my partner asked me whether I had finished the paper front and back. I was like "wait what?" but when I turned the paper, I could see my mom beating me to hell. I was like what to do, I asked my partner how many minutes were remaining. He was like "dude there are only 5 minutes remaining". My hopes drowned as I walked past the school gate towards my mom. She asked the question "how was the paper?". I gave one of the most unexpected answers. "Black and White".

Later as usual I got a slap and I said I fared badly. From the school till we reached home my mom kept on pinching my leg on the bike. It looked like my leg was a DJ mixer and she was the DJ. I was crying and to stop her doing that I used to shake the bike so she could focus on the road but that failed. Before it could get any worse my friend who is a scholar sitting on another bike shouted “the paper was so easy but I got minus 5 on the paper”. I told my mom “saw, he got minus 5”. She didn’t care about it and kept the mixer continuing. That’s when I started hating the scholar. When the results were out, I got 9 out of 50 in that paper but I passed the class miraculously rather to say I didn’t know it was mass promotion. The sad fact was, everyone said “DUDE, DO YOU HAVE A FUTURE?” “GO START COLLECTING PLASTIC BAGS” but during this tough time it was my mom who truly believed in me.

Class 6 and 7 felt like normal days. In Class 8, I joined 'The Boy Scouts' since it was very interesting. In the month of February 2015, we attended a scout’s camp. It was held in an open, wide area surrounded by a forest with a stream nearby. We reached in the afternoon at around 12 noon. The first day we had to set up our tent and make some stuff using sticks like a shoe rack, clothes hanger, chair etc. Later we had lunch and took a siesta. When we got up, we were introduced to 2 people who thought us how to use a zip line in case of an emergency. The zip line is a pulley attached to a cable which is fixed to two trees, both on the either side of the stream. After that we jumped in the stream to have bath and believe me the water was very cold but later, we got used to it. In the night we were given no instructions as in what we should do, never the less we started roaming everywhere until we got a call for dinner and headed towards our tent. Actually, we didn’t sleep instead we along with the kids from the other tents started playing truth and dare later to which we stopped when heard the teachers inspecting the

tents. One of the tent members was dared to perform a pole dance, the moment he started dancing, the teachers entered as if it was a raid. When the teachers came in our tent I prayed not to laugh or smile because if I did, I was sure to be dead.

The next morning, we woke up at around 5:30am and started jogging, stretching and getting our body ready because we had to go trekking. After having breakfast, we left for trekking and I guess I must have been stupid for buying one of the heaviest shoes for a 10km trek, yes, I know that's me. We had gone to a waterfall which was very beautiful. It's an unbelievable moment wherein I went with shoes and came back with them but not on my legs, they were in my hands. Later we had lunch since everyone was starving to death. After getting up we started playing some of our childhood games like 'dog and the bone' and 'Kho Kho'. After which we jumped in the stream to have bath but when we came out of the stream, we were astonished to see our principal who had come to visit us. We clicked a group picture and got back to our work since we had to prepare for our upcoming fire camp program which was at 9pm. Everyone had a done a very a great job in giving their message. Everyone had gone to sleep but one of the unexpected things happened which brought a terror to everyone. Around 3:30am there was a thunderstorm; our tents were almost wet and to our luck we found one bus but we were around 120 students so you can imagine what time we had gone through. In the morning, the teacher congratulated every scout for not panicking and being so disciplined. Around 1pm we reached back to the school.

Class 9 was the worst experience because we had to answer our second semester exams and I remember I had a pain in my stomach area. I entered the class and to my bad luck I was on the first bench. It was almost half an hour, the pain in my stomach was getting worse. I kept on praying until it

got to level which is saved to my long-term memory. All of a sudden, in the middle of deep silence of the examination hall I released a fine noise... POINKK!!!!!! A laughter busted out in the examination hall and everyone knew who did it. I innocently asked my friend "Who did?" he screamed and said "You did". At the end of the day the incident of my fart was preached to the entire school.
Class 10 has been a milestone in my life. At the end of the year everyone knew that I'm not good at studies so they started saying the same thing "Dude, DO YOU HAVE A FUTURE?" "YOU ARE USELESS". I used to save it until one day, the class had planned to visit the aids home for children. The teachers told us to prepare for it, as we had only one month. The boys went to each class personally and asked if anyone was interested in performing a skit at the aids home. They also informed us that it would be held after class. At this moment, I wasn't sure about anything but I had 2 options in my mind either take it or waste it. I called up my mom and told her that I'm participating in a skit, she was very excited about it and supported me. I decided to take it instead but there were a lot of boys, from which some said no since they couldn't wait after class. The script was written, it was a comedy skit and the boys were casted. Unfortunately, I was casted as a side actor, I was very disappointed but I never gave up that part. It was only 10 seconds on stage. All of a sudden, the main actor was not feeling well so he had to be temporarily replaced by someone else. They called me for the main role but they always said "Don't worry, once he comes you will get your part back". I thought to myself "JASON, THIS IS YOUR ONLY CHANCE, FORGET ABOUT EVERYTHING THEY SAID AND GIVE IT YOUR BEST SHOT" and I did. I was casted as the main character for the skit at the aids home. We did the skit so well that we were called upon by the head mistress who informed us that our skit had been selected for the

upcoming annual day. In our school, children who did not participate were not allowed to attend the annual day since it was for parents only, instead they were shown it a few days in advance. I still remember the smiles and laughter on their faces. It kept me motivated. We got a response from the principal saying "THIS WAS THE BEST ACT AND JASON YOU HAVE DONE A GREAT JOB; THE WHOLE SHOW WAS ON YOU". I couldn't feel happier to see my teachers and few parents appreciating my mom. Mom almost cried. Appreciating my mom as she was always there for me when I was down and always supported me in everything I do and she truly deserves it.

At the end of the semester, one of my friends gave me a letter saying that he was sorry for making fun of me and predicting that I wouldn't do anything in life. I hugged him and said "please, don't treat anyone else the way you treated me". He apologized and even asked me if I could join his group for a dinner after the passing out parade. Passing out parade is a solemn occasion held in the evening on the schoolground for Class 10 students. When we were moving out, in a solemn manner I saw the projector lit with pictures from the 5th to 10th. Suddenly a tear dropped from my eye, that's moment I saw every student crying. When we went back to our classroom, I saw the class full of people but yet silence. Everyone including the teacher cried.

A small message to the children reading this "PLEASE ENJOY YOUR, SCHOOL MEMORIES AND DON'T BE AFRAID OF FAILURES BECAUSE WINNING DOSEN'T TEACH YOU ANYTHING BUT FAILURES DO. DON'T CARE ABOUT GOSSIPERS, THEIR JOB IS TO JUST GOSSIP, INSTEAD DO SOMETHING IN LIFE THEY WILL QUICKLIY SHUT THEIR MOUTH. IN THE PAST EVERYONE SAID I WILL NEVER DO ANYTHING IN LIFE AND NOW I'M (A CO-AUTHOR, A MUSICIAN, A

SONGWRITER, A POET AND A SINGER) JUST WORK HARD AND KEEP PRAYING.

"[“A Failure Only Becomes A Failure When One Decides To Give Up”] - JASON DIAS

Taniya Khemchandani

Taniya Khemchandani is an ordinary girl from the city Kota.Her hobbies are singing and writing.She loves to observe things in her life.She is passionate about writing and expressing her feelings into words.

You can contact her through
Instagram: @taniyakhemchandani
Facebook:
Taniya khemchandani
Snapchat:
Iamtaniyaaaaa
Twitter:
@IamTaniyaaaaa
Gmail:
taniyakhemchandani@gmail.com

School ke wo din

School ke kya din the wo jab hum subhe jaldi uthke tayyar hoke (kabhi kabhi bina nahaye) school jate the, wo dost, wo pehla pehla pyaar, wo teachers pe jokes marna, school mai tables bajana, pagalpanti karna.
Kash wo din waapis laut sakte!!
Class mai masti thi
Humari Bhi kuch hasti thi
Teacher ka sahara tha
Dil yeh awaara tha
Kahan aa gaye is duniya ke
Chakkar mein
Wo school hi kitna pyaara tha
Ek tiffin mai 8 haath hua karte the
Hum saare dost tab saath hua karte the
Vo last bench par bethna
Vo first period mai khana
Vo recess mai games
Har pal ek dusre se lada karte the
Hum saare dost tab saath hua karte the
Vo homework wale bahane
Vo teacher ke taane
Vo hamari matargashti
Vo hamari grand masti
Computer lab mai jana
Washroom ka naam leke pure school ka chakkar lagana
Assembly mai na jane ke liye bahane banaye karte the
Hum Sare dost tab saath hua karte the
Kaash! wo din lautkar aa jate
Hum hamare purane roop mai dal jate
Door hoke duniya ke in riwaazo se
Hum firse humari jannat mai jaa pate

School memories

- Polishing white shoes with chalk.
- Hoping that PT days aren't holidays.
- Checking if teacher comes with answer sheet after exams.
- Dreaming about birthday & new clothes for months.
- Keeping quite when principle passes by classroom.
- Hiding behind friends when teacher asks questions.
- First love
- Sleeping with books

First day:

We cry because we don't wanna enter in school.

Last day:

We cry because we don't wanna leave school.

Highschool

Drama & fight, laugh & tears, breakups and makeups. It's rushing to grow up, then realizing you want your innocence. It's hurting over someone else. It's getting drunk and having your best friends hold your hair back as you puke, then re capping your night the next morning. It's jealous and envy, rumours & gossips. It's getting knocked over again & again to the point where you question if you should just stay down. It's disappointment and lies. It's those night where you want to be alone, but you don't want to feel alone.

A fake smile forced upon your face for so long, people actually believe you're happy. It's getting backstabbed & feeling betrayed. It's hearing lie after lie so you learn to never trust anyone but yourself. It's tears on your cheeks that you want to be wiped away by one person, the person who made you cry in the first place.

It's growing up, meeting new people. It's moving on in time, lots & lots of time. It's wishing bad things onto people out of anger. It's hope for a happy future. It's learning and discovering new things. It's hurting but still trying. It's learning from the past mistakes & it's laughing over you someone you once cried over. It's getting stronger, becoming independent. It's seeing you can & are happy at your own.

So, what is High school? It's realization you're so young, carefree and having fun. A whole future at your feet. So maybe it hurts but that's life. Don't listen to everything you hear & take chances, even if it risks getting hurt. Smile & mean it because in 30 years from now you're going to look back on those years you rushed & all you will want is high school.

One day

One day you will be at your last Friday games period. One day you will be at your last game with your team. One day you will be taking your last test and eating your last school lunch. One day you will have your last report card. One day you will have your last young and wild Saturday night with people you have made a million memories with. One day you will be standing in an alphabetical ordered line in a cap and gown with people who you watched grow up. People who watched you grow up. Some of those people you will never see again or hear about. One day you will forget about all the people you knew and you will barely remember the memories until you find a picture that makes you think of one. One day you will be packing up 18 years of your life into boxes and hugging your parent's goodbye. It's sad.... One day you won't be in high school anymore......And we are all ready to leave so soon.

Tulika Singh

Hello friends lets meet with Tulika Singh residing at Ghaziabad, U.P. She is a proficient teacher of English, freelance content writer, Prabhakar in classical vocal from Prayag Sangeet Samiti, Allahabad. She is a social activist of 'Agaaz Sewa Samiti Trust'. She is also a business woman. She has keen interest in oration and recitation of poems both in English and Hindi. Followed by Mental Health Advisor from Agra hospital and from Ranchi (RINPAS). She has bagged these credentials due her lovable God, mentors, parents and her better-half, who is always there by her side to support her, encourage her now and forever.

GOLDEN MEMORIES OF SCHOOL

'School is a daily routine for us. In the morning, we're sure to make a fuss.
Even when the sun is still not up.
Here we are, awake at 5 am sharp.'
We all have a tendency to provoke our mind by saying that school life is quite boring wherein every day is the same day right from waking up early in the morning till sleeping tight at night and again we are scheduled with our class lectures, completing homework, submitting our assignments on time and preparing for exams at night.
Am I right children?
Every single day is a rush-rush moment from school to coaching and then leading towards our residence. "I sometimes ask questions to myself what is so great in going to school every day? Oh God! It is torture for me all day long."
I can't forget those days when my eyes were half open, shoelace undone and entering to the school gate half panting in the last moment before our school prayer begun but as soon as I use to see my friends, I tend to forget all my fears of getting scolding from teachers and wear a smile on my face along with my friends. I am sure you all must have faced the same situations. Right?
I remember the funniest moment of my school life was having lunch in the midst of lectures which was followed by the reprimanding of my dear teachers.
Well, I believe teachers are skillful in spying their students' mischiefs and have full knowledge of our deeds which serves as a helping instrument to scold us in the class with their same dialogues over and over again. "Let's meet our beloved hooligan of our class who will bring laurels to our school without studying but by showing her mischiefs in the class.

Let's clap for our brightest student of the year TULIKA DEY."

Gosh! Such an embarrassing moment for me, still use to giggle as if I had done something really honourable.

Let me guess how many of you can really relate this moment? I guess many of you.

Isn't it quite memorable and Aha moment for all of us? Although we should not do this.

When I ponder seriously then I found that we were really very mischievous students to be handled by our lovely teachers. They boar our mischiefs, still taught us smilingly and helped us. They were ready to listen and acted friendly. Their hard work paid off when we reached our nineth cloud. I feel school life is as sweet as sugar for all of us. We had learnt so much with action

Such as camps, experiments, concerts and activities. We had learned so much and save the tress.

Some may see school as a torture chamber,
Some cannot wait for holidays in December,
But it depends on how we look at school.
Honestly, positively, school is cool!

THE DAY I SOARED HIGH LIKE AN EAGLE

"All Great Achievements
Require TIME"
By MAYA ANGELOU.

Yes, precisely I do agree with the statement. All fruits need some time to ripen. If you cannot wait till it gets ripen then the result is just a zero.

Patience, dedication, persistence and self-belief bring achievement in your life. For that you need to strive hard in order to reach your Final Destination.

Friends are you interested to know how did I achieve? Let's hop in the Time Machine to know my story. It is the story when I was in my teens. I was extremely introvert girl and barely talked to anyone. I never felt the requirement of any pals to share my thoughts or my feelings with others. Those were not the days of having even online friends. I enjoyed hearing class lecture of teachers and engrossed totally in studies.

My school days were filled with down in terms of socialization before they became ups.

I was insecure and had complexities, had no friends until I developed my own self-esteem through my creative writings, orations, recitation of poems and singing on the stage. I accuse and abuse myself before all these co curriculum activities held in my alma mater.

I considered myself as an unattractive, obese lass with low confidence in my pocket. I stuttered before initiating any conversations to my teachers and classmates. I had no clue what to do next to change my personality.

I took help from my parents and teachers too but I was failed to satisfy myself with right answers and sat aloof! Those thoughts were showing its grin teeth to me all the time and so had sleepless night and a bagful of nightmares which affected my studies altogether.

Guys we all are aware from our social mediums whose petty and useless questions haunts you all night like a monster but

can't do anything as its still prevails in our stereotypical society.
One fine day, my mind pops up with an idea to chuck my negative trash feelings and to count my abilities to transform "ME".
TULIKA started orating, reciting poems and shared her creative writings on the stage. She was too glad and danced in glee that she came to know her instilled ability of jotting things on paper but she again flashed with a challenge and that was her fright to speak in front of the public. She somehow took the challenge and mustered some courage to please the audiences presenting her work through the stage performances. Firstly, she was scared enough, had goosebumps all over her hands, felt thirsty before uttering a word followed by butterflies in her stomach. She just closed her eyes, prayed to Almighty God and started delivering her speech.
And guess what?
With a spur of a moment audiences got carried away by her performance and started applauding loud which gave wings to me to fly high in the sky. I was totally awestruck to see my POWER lively.
And yes, from that day onwards I never looked back and soared high like an eagle till now.
Somebody from the audience shouted at her top of her voice and said,
"SUCCESS IS FAILURE TURNED INSIDE OUT,
SO, STICK TO THE FIGHT WHEN YOU'RE HARDEST HIT.
REST IF YOU MUST, BUT DON'T YOU QUIT."
From then I became the twinkling star of my ALMA MATER and had FRIENDS to share my thoughts with them.
It definitely took some time to change me but if the result is positive then why not I should wait?
Do you agree with me?

THE BEST SHIP OF ALL IS FRIENDSHIP

The most beautiful relationship of everyone's life in school days are our FRIENDS FOREVER.

I always felt speechless what friends meant to me and how important they are to me. For me pals are my stress buster and they are as necessary as my body parts. Yes, earlier I regretted for barely having friends but now it's a Aha moment for me after I soared high in the sky.

Words are getting short to describe my feelings regarding my friends but I tried to portray my token of love through this poem. I hope you will all like it. Stanzas are like this:

"Friendship is priceless
And can never be forgotten
Friendship is timeless
And never be rotten.
It takes more than hugs and kisses
To be real friend.
The nature of friendship
Requires a blend.
The road to a happy life
May sometimes makes us stumble
But to have a friend to give us a hand
Teaches us to be humble.
Good friends are hard to find,
Hard to lose,
And impossible to forget
But when they fly away,
Your anger turns to regret.
Sometimes in life we need a special person
To listen while we talk.
A special person who will not
Discourage or judge
But encourage as we walk.

Friends are there
To help you long.
In life,
There are big ships,
And there are small ships,
But the best ship of all
Is friendship."

I hope I am not wrong in showcasing the beauty of this relationship. What do you say?

GUIDING LAMPS OF MY LIFE

GURU BRAHMA
GURU VISHNU
GURU DEVO MAHESHWARA
GURU SHAKSHAT PARAMBRAHMA
TASMAYE SHRI GURUVE NAMAH.

Such true and pious lines are iterated of our Gurus. Teachers are the creators of young minds, they are the real functional body of our society, they are humble, noble and modest like Lord Shiva who take cares of their students no matter what. I bow my heads with folded hands and pray to god for giving us such a wonderful nation builder in our life to give them strength and energy to live long forever.

Teachers are always my backbone and foreteller of my future who had prophesied about my potentials before I took myself seriously.

Through this writing, I would like to thank all my education-shapers who tried utmost to back me with confidence in my oddities of life.

"The night has been unruly. Where we lay,
Our chimneys were blown down . . .
Some say the Earth
Was feverous and did shake."

These are the famous lines taken from Macbeth which actually applied in my life. How? Well, when I was facing the torments within me all hopes shattered just the same way as happened in Macbeth but my Lady Macbeth (mentors) helped me face that chaos which was within me and tried to blow down my unpleasant thoughts regarding me that was not that easy as it seems to be but their counselling gave me the power to bring change even in my odd weather.

Friends we never gave significance to our education builders and when we do understand it becomes too late. I feel worthy enough to have humble gurus in all my pathways. My gurus knew me better than anyone else.

Behind every success our teachers and preachers play a pivotal role to put everything in sync in our life. They selflessly gave their hands to transform my personality. They were the one who appraised

Me as a 'PERSON' first and then 'MY WORK'. I had never let them down. I had underestimated my caliber but mentors use to gear my throttle and lend their helping hands to grow. I can connect myself to a small seed who grows up tall and finishes in blooming trees and all this happened due to the love and support of the gardener of our life(teachers).

I was the toughest person to change my entire persona but actually a vote of thanks goes to our gardener who had never said ugh! While shaping us and continuously put an effort to make us a strong tree. In short, they are my angels, they have so much of POWER, PATIENCE and BELIEF on ME that one day I will be a shining star who will also set a ray of light and hope like our teachers do and will never ask anything in return from you.

Nowadays mentors are working like corona warrior apart from their mundane chores, they are preparing presentations in their best possible way to teach their students from home no matter what so that their little stars do wonders in their life. I salute those teachers who are working all day long, learnt computer to work from their home on meagre salary putting a smile on their face. Today if I am here with my credentials, it's because of their efforts. Teachers are always on their duty teaching every day in a new way. I admire few of my teachers a lot. Our teachers are next to our mothers who understand their students well and help them selflessly. For teachers their reward is only when their students come up with their flying colours in their life. I have understood this well when I am on their shoelace.

Do you remember the shining star of Bihar, A TEACHER, named as Anand Kumar of the remarkable movie SUPER 30? That's what the teachers are.

BIDDING AN ADIEU TO YOUR ALMA MATER

No matter which every phase of life you're in, you'll agree that nothing ever beats school life. And that's why bidding goodbye to your school is no easy feat. Bidding an adieu to your alma mater is the hardest and most emotional days of lives in school.

It is a blend of happiness and sadness. Happiness of stepping ahead to face the new challenges of life and sadness of leaving behind your friends and your carefree life.

It is the day when we are overloaded with past memories of our carefree days. During those days we forget all our rivals and prepare ourselves before the mirror taking a chit in our hand to present a farewell speech and the song on the stage addressing your principal, teachers' classmates, school and friends.

Moreover, I usually sit back on the couch sipping a cup of tea and ponder how much I use to admire my school uniform and feel proud to be the part of my alma mater. It looks like a gratified wall. Your juniors, friends and teachers use to give their autographs, fill your slam books to treasure it in your heart. Those were the real emotions which are always at brink and would love to cherish and relish all over again in my life.

My school life ends up in 30 seconds of farewell song and exchange of speeches and vote of thanks from teachers and schoolmates with a bucket full of tears, hugging everyone and wishing them good luck for our near future and teachers giving tips to success. On the other hand, eating platterful of food stuffs and clicking pictures from every corner of the school with friends and teachers to treasure it in our heart forever.

These are all immortal feelings which never fades away with an hour but refreshes our soul when we recollect these memories of school having school albums on one hand.

That was my beautiful experiences of my school life. What about you? Share your views if possible.

Jesvita Princy Quadras

Jesvita Princy Quadras is a 22-year-old girl from the coastal city of Mangalore, Karnataka. She has been working for catholic youth of the country for over 5 years. Thus, she aspires to work for the youth of the country as a career choice too. She loves to write and her writing comes from her personal experience. She wishes to be a counsellor and someday help children and adolescents of their various conflicts. She believes her greatest achievement to be her meeting the Pope in 2019.
Get to know more about her on Instagram: 98_jq

Echo of the Desk

I hear an echo
That whispers to me
The sound of chitter chatter
The sound of mirth and laugh
The sound of hymns and choirs
The sound of mid breaks that go silent
The sound of tables and skits and dancing
The sound of bitterness between 'girlies'
The sound of sisters and teachers and cabinet ministers!
The sound of gossips and fashion sense talks
You may wonder what all this sound is about?
Well, don't stress my dear
It speaks of the place I grew up in
The place that taught me how important morning prayer is
The place that taught me how important reciting the school and national anthem is
The place where I heard my true calling
The place that taught me that girls can be mean and the sweetest all at the same time.
The place that groomed me to be the person I am today!

If you got a little idea by the poem, it would mean you know where I studied. Yup, in a convent school. Super disciplined, strictly English and uniformity is a must.

Anyways this isn't where I would want to begin my story at. I was actually born into a huge family in a small village called Shirva in Udupi district in the south. Till my UKG I went to the school in my village and I made friends. More than girls I had boy- best friends.

If you ask why, it was because I was the boss lady in my class. And that is because my mother was a teacher in the

same school. I was a pet of all the teachers. I had the privilege to write my exams in the headmistress's office. I had the privilege of getting all birthday chocolates and laddus from all the other teachers. My boy best friends taught me to climb trees and windows. All the mischief that was instilled in me, well thanks to them.

But as my Pappa was abroad he decided we move to the nearest city for better education. Fun fact: I had super long hair till my UKG. But my mom who had zero idea of tying one's hair told me that the new school requires only short hair and I had to chop my hair and alas what a boy I looked like!

2004, the year we moved to this great but small city of Mangalore. The first round around the city made me think I was in a foreign country. Lame but adorable, alright? A new house, a new school, a new life, all in a new city. Excited but a tinge of fear.

The first day of school wasn't the best day of school for me. Like most of the kids I too had tears in my eyes. But not because I knew no one there. It was because I along with three other kids were the only ones with boy cut hair. Yup, mom bluffed. And I had no option but to live with it for the rest of my life. (kidding… just till my 8th grade)

Frankly speaking, it wasn't easy. Especially because I was a village girl in a city. I thought we moved outside India to be frank. That was how I saw the new city to be. Also, in my new school all the other girls were already introduced to each other and I had no friends for one entire year.

The second year I found my calling. That turned out to be singing. So, since my second grade I was known for singing. Sadly, I was not allowed to explore anymore talents. I wanted to be a part of the drama, dance and other activities too.

But I'm sure most of you all who are average or below in studies have experienced that only the toppers get that. I

didn't even know that I could write. But the credit for my fluency in language goes to my school English teachers and of course because it was a convent school. If we didn't speak in English we were fined.
And therefore, I was known for singing and singing alone. It may be a competition, morning assembly, recordings or whatever it maybe the name JESVITA always popped in. Okay not boasting alright! Getting to the serious part.
Sadly, our school was the kind that favoured the toppers only. I was literally marked with an L that stands for LOSER on my forehead for scoring less in a class test when I was just 8. I told you, I wasn't a topper.
But interestingly all of my friends were toppers. That became the reason for me to be left out always. If you ask why? Well, because my topper friends were always around the teachers to help them in one or the other way. Be it studies or extra curriculars.
What's more interesting is that despite the favouring I was made a part of the school council both in primary an in high school. (at the same time threatened to be thrown out of the council if I didn't score well). If I see the positive version of me having topper friends, my notes were always complete and I had all the help I could get in the name of studies.
Fun fact: I was also one of the laziest in the class. This explains why I could never top, I guess. My teachers always said that I had the ability but my laziness got in the way. I slept a LOT in school. Not to forget how I was slow in eating my afternoon lunch. I had the smallest lunch box in class but damn that bell. It always rang before I could finish my food. As a result, I was made to sit on the stairs almost every day until I finished my lunch box and showed it to the teacher in charge.
So basically, school life wasn't always fun and frolic. There were hard times and sometimes even harder times. But the hardest times was when I left alone to live.

I mentioned about me knowing that girls can be the sweetest and the meanest at the same time. Like I said I had a lot of friends. Mostly toppers. We had wonderful time together. Did I mention that I was this humorous girl too? So basically, they study, they taught me and I kind of entertained them.
But! Of course, there's a 'but' here. There were times when my emotions got out of hand. I couldn't help but cry bitterly. Initially I told them the reasons. But eventually they got sick and tired of it. That was when their mean side would pop out. Well, that explains why I had harder times in school.
Oh, how could I forget. I composed this amazing song for myself which I kept singing every time I would get a chance to. It goes something like this:
"I am the batman.
Who can be as strong as strong as me?"
That's it! The word 'composed' seemed to have heightened your expectations huh? This song would crack up anyone anywhere. Oh yes. This song came in with actions too. I had my fist held out to others with the sign of the batman drawn on it.
Moving on for my 11th and 12th grade I had to move to another school. That is when my contact with almost everyone broke down. But I did have one person rom my high school who was with me in my pre university days. Oh, the times we had were so lovely. Our class was small so everyone was close to everyone in the class. However, I couldn't quite create an identity here. It was because our school was one of the top institutes of my city and there were thousands of students. This was also a convent school.
This place is where I found my true calling of career that I would choose. I actually thought that I'd end up being a teacher or a lecturer like my mother. But who knew that my calling would take me to a totally different steam. I opted the subject before I could join the pre university. Learning was fun. I got promoted from being a student who was average

or below to a student above average and borderline topper. Although I couldn't really understand the difference.
Towards the end of my second year a few known singers found me and asked to join their band for a competition. I was super thrilled. I had never been a part of any bands you know. For me and I guess for you as well, 16-17 are bitter stages of life. You are no more a child and not an adult too. The task of trying to fit in is your goal. I failed miserably.
I realised that only time would help me with the same. One may wonder why I jumped from being a part of a band to identity crisis. Being in the band made me realise I'm not as talented as I thought I would be. The other members in the group were so much better. And I had to practically live in between them for months of practise which made it worse.
They were all already close to one another. When they realised that I didn't have the potential to be with them it was already too late. Therefore, they gave me no part to sing but a person who sings along in a chorus. I mean how could they kick me out right?
Once the band days were over, I was back in class only to find that my one friend had already made new friends and I was left behind. Luckily only a month of class was remaining. And I lived through it quite impressively. Next was college. Again, I found a person from my 11th and 12th and we grew close in no time. The first year was the hardest because I was caught up in an emotional state. But my class was the best. Not only did many come forward to help but many others became friends with me despite my condition.
The next three years were truly the best. I found friends who accepted me the way I am and vice versa. They became my family. Literally. And I thank them for the same.
This reminds of what my high school principal used to tell us every day. "high school days will be noted down as the three golden years of your life."

Well for me it was high school but college days. Although I will cherish both my school and college days altogether.
As I end this write up, I want to add something cliché but something that's important. My gratefulness towards my teachers and mentors. My gratefulness towards my friends and foes. My gratefulness towards those who spoke to me only on my birthdays to get a chocolate from me and ignored me the rest of the time. My gratefulness towards everyone I came across since my 1st grade to my 12th grade.

I'm sorry that you had to read a lot of sadness than happiness. But hey, isn't life a struggle from the start. Since childhood we try really hard to fit in. Some do and some don't.
My story is of the don't. Many of you may sympathise or even empathise with my sharing. However, I can say that I'm in a much better place today.
I may have gained my identity today through other means but my childhood will never repeat itself. However, I still choose to be grateful towards the people I mentioned earlier. They taught me to be strong in their own way.
Not the best way but their own way. I often wonder what if I was a topper? What if I had longer hair in school? What if the teachers liked me for who I was and not for who they wanted me to be? What if my friends had never left me alone on the thorny path?
What if? I wonder!

Shabeena Khatoon

Co-author Shabeena Khatoon is a Student at Delhi University pursuing Bachelor's degree. She considers her faith and family to be the most important to her. She is fond of reading books, quotes, poems, motivational stories etc. She is a good writer and she loves to write her own thoughts in an adorable way. She wants to contribute her efforts in the development of her own country and also wants to make her parents proud.

Ig:- @heaven_writes_2020

स्कूल की याद : एक मुलाक़ात

क्यों न आज पुराने दिनों से मुलाक़ात की जाए,
एक-एक यादों के मोती से, माला पिरोई जाए।
क्यों न उन पलों को ताज़ा किया जाए,
एक बार फिर, उन लम्हों को जीने का इरादा किया जाए।।
पहनी थी न्यू यूनिफॉर्म हमने, बड़े खुश होकर,
नन्ही सी मुस्कान थी, उस मासूम चेहरे पर।
था कंधे पर बस्ता और थी गले में बोतल,
घर से निकले थे हम, माँ का हाथ थामकर।।
पहुँचे थे, जब स्कूल गेट पर,
माँ तो जा रही हैं, ये सोचकर...
काजल वाली आँखो में, आ गई थी आँसुओ की लहर।
लेकिन इस बात की मुझे बहुत खुशी थी,
कि रोने वाली आँखें, सिर्फ़ मेरी नही थी,
और हमे रोता देख, सामने खड़ी टीचर भी हँस रही थी।।
भीगी-भीगी आँखों समेत, कक्षा में बिठाया गया,
रफ्ता-रफ्ता, ज्ञान का दीपक भी जलाया गया।
दिन बीतते गए और दोस्त भी बनते गए,
कुछ जुड़ते गए, तो कुछ बिछड़ते गए।।
पहली, दूसरी, तीसरी, चौथी, पाँचवी,
एक-एक करके सब पार करते गए।
गिरते – पड़ते ही सही, नई-नई चीज़ें सीखते गए,
लेकिन चाहे कुछ भी हो, वो वक्त बड़ा सुहाना था,
अलग सी दुनिया थी, अलग सा ज़माना था।
अगर दोस्त रूठ जाए, तो अब्बा-कुट्टा कहकर मनाना था,
दिल में कोई मतभेद नहीं था,सबके पास वक्त भी खूब था।।
बात ये तब की हैं,
जब क्लासरूम से टॉयलेट का रास्ता तो सीधा होता था।

लेकिन टॉयलेट से क्लासरूम का रास्ता,
भूलभुलैय्या से कम नहीं होता था।।
सुबह सुबह, स्कूल जल्दी जाना,
और फिर, पहली सीट के लिए लड़ना।
अपने लंच मे क्या हैं, इससे ज़्यादा,
दोस्त क्या लाया हैं, इसकी फिक्र करना,
लंच भले ही एक हो, उसमें हाथ तो चार दिखते थे,
अब क्या ही बताऊं,उन पलों के अलग ही मज़े थे।।
छठी, सातवीं, आठवी, नवी का सफ़र भी खत्म हो चुका था,
धीरे धीरे हम बड़े हो रहे थे,
दसवीं के मैदान में कदम भी रख चुके थे,
अब तक तो बस हमने, ट्रेलर देखा था,
असल में मूवी तो अब शुरू हुई थी,
ज़िंदगी भी, क्या खूब मज़े ले रही थी,
क्योंकि इस साल, कई दोस्त जुदा हो गए थे,
साइंस, कॉमर्स, ह्यूमैनिटीज के आधार पर बंट गए थे।
सबके रास्ते अलाहिदा हो गए थे।।
ज़िंदगी के एक नए पन्ने में दाखिल हो रहे थे।
आंखों में सपने भी कुछ कम बड़े नही थे।।
स्कूललाइफ के आख़िरी मक़ाम पर, पहुँच चुके थे,
ज़िंदगी के खेल से पुरी तरह अंजान थे,
कौन अपना हैं, और कौन पराया, ये अब पता चल रहा था,
हर इंसान का, एक नया चेहरा सामने आ रहा था।।
बड़े तो हो रहे थे, लेकिन दिल तो आख़िर! बच्चा ही था,
टीचर के नए-नए नाम तो अब भी रखते थे।
और उनके न आने की खुशी में शोर भी मचाते थे,
क्लास में कुछ कलाकार तो ऐसे थे,
जो टीचर की नक़ल तक उतारते थे।।
पिकनिक की यादें और क्रश से जुड़ी बाते तो रह ही गई,
इसके बिना तो स्कूललाईफ ऐसी हैं,

जैसे सब्ज़ी में नमक का न होना...
मना करने के बाद भी, छुपाकर फ़ोन ले जाना,
पिकनिक का मेन्यू तैयार करना,
किसको, क्या लाना हैं, ये बताना।
चलती बस में अंताक्षरी और डांस के लुत्फ़ उठाना,
गाने के मौके पर, इज़हार का चौका लगाना,
आप समझ ही गए होंगे, अब इसके आगे क्या ही बताना।।
एक तरह से देखा जाए, तो पूरी स्कूललाइफ थी, बेमिसाल...
फेयरवेल की मस्ती भी थी, कमाल...
लेकिन कही न कही सबकी आँखें थी, नम...
स्कूल छूट जाएगा, सबको था इसी बात का गम...
सफर का आगाज़ हुआ था, आंसुओ से...
सफर का अंत हुआ, आंसुओ पर...
जितना बताया जाए, उतना हैं, कम...
कुछ ऐसी हैं, इस लम्बे सफ़र की डगर।।
जैसे-जैसे वक्त बीता, सब पीछे छूटता गया,
बस रह गया, मन के अंदर, यादों का बलखाता समन्दर।
फिलहाल, तो बस यही हैं, तमन्ना...
बस मिल जाए, उन दिनो में वापस जाने का कोई बहाना।
हाँ! माना कि, थी बंदिशे...
लेकिन वो था एक अलग ही ज़माना।।
अंत में...!!!
सबकी ज़बान पर बस यही शब्द रह जाते है,
काश! वो पल, वो दिन, एक बार फिर वापस आ पाते,
काश! एक बार फिर हम माँ की ऊंगली थाम, स्कूल जा पाते,
काश! एक बार फिर वही यूनिफॉर्म पहन, कक्षा में बैठ पाते।
खुदा हम पर एक बार फिर मेहरबान हों जाए,
काश! एक बार फिर वो तक़दीर हमे वापस मिल जाए।।
काश!...!!!

Palak Tanwar

Palak Talwar is an ambitious writer in her early 20s. She is a master's student with efficient writing skills. She has done her graduation in English literature from University of Delhi and is a proficient writer in diverse topics ranging from lifestyle to technical writing. Having interned in various well-known companies, she is currently a sub editor of a magazine. You can connect her on LinkedIn: https://www.linkedin.com/in/palak-talwar-a8610a145/ and also mail her at palaktalwar4@gmail.com

Personified School Memories

School used to be the most boring times of our lives but equally fun too. Now, when we look back to our class photograph, there is a nostalgic scent to it and imperishable memories of all the tiny bits of fun that turned into a ball of amusement. Our precious memories are bound to be made and fade with time.

From having 'stomach aches' in the morning to impatiently waiting for the last bell to ring, the eight hours of school seemed never-ending. Yet, now when I go down memory lane, all I think about is the fun I had.

Some school memories are engraved into our hearts so much that we still find ourselves grinning and cherishing the flashbacks. The last page of our books used to be our creative corner, playing tick-tack-toe in free period and doodling whatever came to our mind in the utmost dull periods used to give us eternal bliss.

Constantly checking if we will end up with our crush using FLAMES and taking the longest routes to the washroom, praying that the bell might ring now, were the kind of excitements that cannot be matched with anything else.

The only fights we ever had were on who gets to sit behind the smartest kid in class during exams.

We all have lots of good and bad memories associated with school, and now when I think about my school life, some incidents spread a smile on my face, like sitting on the backbench to sleep during maths class and asking a tall kid to 'cover' me while escaping the assembly. I also remember opening my lunch box in the middle of the periods because apparently, the lunch break seemed too far away.

I still remember the very first day I stepped into a new school with my twin brother. We both were in the same section until

our streams separated us in 11th grade. My twin brother and I possess different personalities. He was a chill and more excellent kid in school, whereas I was an introvert and sort of a dull kid.

As a child, I always used to compare myself to my twin brother. Being the total opposite of my twin, I used to be anxious about literally everything, ranging from attending classes to doing my homework. I was an average student in school and was never fascinated to go to school much. Being passive and emotional was my only hobby, and I used to find solace in sleeping and eating all the time.

Gradually when I grew up, I realised that I have to put meaning to my life and cannot act like a pampered toddler all my life. So, during my high school years, I started building my personality, had a goal in mind, and worked meticulously to achieve it.

With my parent's constant support and encouragement, I attained one of the top three positions in the 12th board exams in the entire school. I was stunned by the results and couldn't believe that my name was among the other two who topped in the whole Humanities stream.

My mother, who is also my first teacher in life, played a crucial role in sculpting my future. She is the pillar of inspiration and support to me. Her life lessons helped me get through school with flying colours.

My teachers played an essential part in making me a better human being. They shaped and polished me so that I become more confident in life and faced all the ups and downs of school life bravely.

Relatable Memories

Some of us found school life tedious, and for others, it was the best period of our lives. However, for some, school life was not an exciting journey, and some would trade anything in a heartbeat for being a child again.

Sooner or later, we realised that school life was a journey that began with tears in our eyes as toddlers being separated from our parents now ended in the same tearful manner, only the separation this time was from those who initially were strangers but ended up being a part of our tinny bubble.

The power of resilience, the strength of togetherness and the never-perishing faith imbibed in us by our school, which impalpably became our second home, will remain with us forever. As I look back now, I am reminded of the tremendous joys and numerous upheavals I went through.

The protective environment of our school made us ready for the unpredictable life ahead. Moreover, the endless perseverance the wealth of knowledge granted to us by our teachers is priceless. Such quantum of teachings acquired from school is applicable everywhere, which helps us to live our lives to the fullest.

I want to conclude by saying….

14 years of school ended long ago,
But the imperishable memories still glow.
Don't hold back on the tears and laughter,
Make fullest of your emotions from hereafter.
Bittersweet memories all started here,
Of happiness, sadness, anger and fear.
It's time to move on as the future comes near,
It's time to put an end to all our smears.

Alas, let us all adore our irreplaceable school memories,
And replenish our hearts with these priceless
ceremonies.

Sakshi Garg Jadhav

"Always follow your dreams, because they will make you feel alive and give meaning to your life - Sakshi Garg Jadhav". Sakshi Garg Jadhav is a post-graduate with a degree in mass communications. She has worked with various corporates and PR agencies for over 7 years and is now a freelance content writer. Residing in the sleepless city of Mumbai with her hubby and loves travelling, reading, and painting. She loves exploring nature and is an adrenaline junkie. A content writer by profession and a cheerful homemaker; she believes that we learn a lot from our situations and surroundings.

THE CORRIDOR OF REMINISCENCE

As I sit down gazing outside my window
I close my eyes…I take a deep breath
Goosebumps all over my body…
Crisp uniforms, bags full of books,
I walk down the corridor giggling with my friends…
We enter the echoing classrooms and throw our bags,
Some more laughs, some more jokes…
Some more wishing for the teacher to be absent…
Gone are those days…
Of boring classes and slumber
Of homework and detention
Of projects and parties
Of tests and grades
Of crushes and flames
Of laughs and quarrels
Where is that wonderful life of friends' paradise?
Those uncomplicated days were just so fine
I miss my school…I miss my friends
And the two seats of the last bench.

JUST A GIRL IN BOARDING SCHOOL

It was class five,
When I was first sent to boarding school.
With an apprehensive heart,
I scuttled through the campus.
The beautiful green mountains,
The mystical waterfalls,
I still remember the mango tree,
That stood near the dorm.
The church bell ringing at six,
The morning chaos full of cliques,
Bonding over breakfast with friends,
That chitter chatter and dirty pranks,
We cross the massive playground,
Just to reach the school.
Sneaking those innocent glances,
As we forget to do our homework.
Gossiping and jabbering with friends,
We pass the day as it ends.
After the afternoon nap,
It is time for study hour.
As the sun goes down,
We struggle to stay awake.
The buzzer rings,
And we take a deep sigh.
Dining together in the mess,
We sit upright with droopy eyes.
The nights are weary and tired,
We slumber into the cozy blanket.
Just to wake in the wee hours,
Those giggles in the pillow,
Those tears under the blanket,
Those fight for one bite Maggie,

How will I ever forget?
The happy talks..
The pillow fights..
The cries turned into smiles..
The dozing off in classroom..
The midnight fun memories..
Boarding became my second home,
Where friends turned into family.

AN ODE TO SCHOOL DAYS

The best years of my life,
I sing along with a fife.
Worth a billion dollars,
Only realized when I became a scholar.
Oh! How can I relive those days,
The blissful and candor phase.
My dreams never had a boundary,
They all have become history.
No matter how old I become,
To those memories, I will always succumb.
Held close to my heart,
Those reminiscences were never apart.
The playful dates with my best friend,
The squabbles that I tried to amend.
I was no teachers' pet,
As homework was I always forget.
Those series of surprise tests,
Always keeping me stressed.
I always had a smile on my face,
That no one could ever replace.
I still remember my first crush,
My cheeks can even now blush.
Trying to look cool in the uniform,
The pigtail that would always deform.
The chuckles that I shared,
That is what I ever cared.
The first fight at the school,
Bullying juniors was the rule.
The first time when I cried,
I found my friends by my side.
The last bench was my habitat,
I made nasty jokes like a brat.

Always waiting for lunch time,
I was always eager to perform a new crime.
Friends are what I always cared,
The strong bond that we shared.
Here is an ode to my school days,
The one that I will always praise.

Preeti Mawri

Preeti Mawri an aspirant young girl who is on the hunt for her flair and love to exhibit her inner self through her writings. She was born and raised in the city of Delhi, basically belongs to the beautiful and heavenly state of Uttarakhand. She prioritize her faith and family. She has always been fascinated by philosophical readings, and this interest has led to some early exposure to writing her own thoughts and write-ups. She conjures up an eclectic, even musing images through the diverse collection of endeavours in her till life and delivers these as lessons learnt which also compel readers to have a thoughtful reading.

The First Bus Ride

Woke up to my momma's voice,
Thinking is it already time to rise.
Momma shouted, "make haste you little nut case", wanna miss the bus on the very first day?
Me full of Zing jumped off my ring. My first bus ride to my first school, isn't it gonna be cool?
Bathed by momma, now dressed too, waiting for bus with 5 others
I can see the bus approaching, A big yellow colour moving box with so many windows
And now as it's getting closer, I don't feel the zest anymore,
All I can feel is butterflies fluttering in my belly and my heart beating like a drum.
As, the bus pulls off in front of me, I don't want to leave momma's hand.
My eyes filling up and head towards ground, my mother asks me not be scared and kisses my warm cheeks.
And slowly made me board on the school bus. Me being coy looked so many new faces staring at me, I start to walk looking for a seat.
Just as I heard a very sweet voice "come sit here", and that instance I got a new friend. Soon, the smiles and bliss around replace my jitters, as I wave goodbye to mommy from my School Bus.

Second Home

Home is where your heart is, and heart dwells where love is. Then how is school our second home? Isn't it the place where we resented and cried to go? Didn't want to leave mommy's hand and walk into a complete strange place with unfamiliar faces.

As time flew by, we never cried and with a glee face we always arrived. With friends we laughed and played mischiefs and at the end it all worth it.

School teachers have their own flair, sometimes strict but always care. They taught us lessons not just from books always imparted beyond our view.

They scolded but solved it at last, they strived to make us a flawless Brat. That concern and love was no less than a parent's those teachers were like our parents.

All the fun and programs we took part in, how unanimously every student worked for it. It made us stronger and brought us together, this is the place we learnt to grow with each other.

How rapid things went by, we cried again when it was our final goodbye.

Hard it is to let go off a family we made over time, that place we lived the best part of our life. The place filled with immense love and memories, it's our Second Home truly.

Friends Forever

Friends, the only family we choose. The best ones are made in school.

They make the school life the best phase, that phase exhibits ups and down but when those friends are around everything is like merry-go-round.

Recess is the part we never miss, we dig in every tiffin.

Every nuisance got me punished, but it's alright with friends too in it.

We partnered for everything whether a function or picnic. We had fights, we had strains but the true ones never got drifted.

School felt fascinated every day, thanks to those friends who were always there.

Innocence of the school gives the most innocent and true friends, Kind of friends we can get nowhere else.

Friendship is the first lesson taught, that is never forgotten all lifelong.

Friends are the most beautiful memories of the school as they are the ones we make those memories with.

Some are lost some are gained, we make numerous along the way.

The school may end but not the bond it gave us Friends that are for life and beyond.

Nostalgia

School days are the best phase of our life. It is the developing period for everyone. They draw our character, mould our mental attitudes and style the basic principles of life. School days fill the mind and heart with nostalgic memories. Countless memories tied with school days.

Time moves in one direction, memories in another!

I still remember the first day in school. It is a common tradition that kids cry continuously on getting separated from their parents. Entering a new environment filled with unfamiliar people caused anxiety.

Learning alphabets and numbers was all easy. Best part was shouting our lungs out while reciting the poetry rhymes to volumes all tuned high.

Zest of buying new school uniform, covering books with brown sheet and pasting your cartoon stickers before every academic year. Going back next year and seeing all the same students. It was so enthusiastic to meet friends, new comers and teachers after a two months long summer vacation and start a new academic year.

Independence Day, Republic Day, Teachers' Day, Childrens' Day, Annual day, sports day, tournaments, cultural meet, debates competitions, writing articles for the school magazine, trips and picnics...all these activities made the school life cheerful, interesting and enjoyable. School time would have been boring without these big celebrations. How much we began to think about wearing a traditional attire for all these different celebrations. All these celebrations were so much fun.

Listening to tediously long speeches from school principal and the guests, standing under the hot sun in schoolyards. Eating the box lunch quickly so that the remaining time could be spent for playing. Free periods were the best thing ever. Everyone

was free to do their own thing. Exchanging amusing gossips on who has a crush on whom, playing love percentage, wearing casuals on your birthday and the whole class singing 'Happy Birthday to you'.

Most importantly, the pillars...Our teachers! They all had lovely and dynamic personalities. They made every student feel joyous. They were the ones who radiated warmth and love. There had been many teachers who had influenced and inspired me.

My school gave me amazing friends, generous and loads of memories to share with others. I just did not realize how soon time passed by. Wish I just rewind time. As we went from high school to college, new college life and friends never came at the expense of school friends. Now a days, platforms like Instagram and WhatsApp always keep us in touch with each other.

Nostalgia is for the times we miss and want to rewind. No matter, Wherever I go... However far away...no one can steal these moments and memories from me.

Arushi Agarwal

Arushi Agarwal, a girl from Kanpur and a freelance writer with an honour's degree in English Literature and currently pursuing masters in English from Savitribai Phule Pune University is trying to know about her life's aim among so many interests she has. She expresses her feeling through different form of arts such as writing, painting, dancing, cooking to name a few. She always tries to write in such a way that it should directly reach to the hearts of people. Hope she is able to do so. She is fond of writing 2 to 4 liners or short stories. To read her Alfaz, you can check her Instagram handle @alfaz_ya_guftugu with a pen name /Aru/.

Life Lesson in School

Giving almost 12 to 14 years of your life to a place is like giving up your most precious moments of life to it. And that place is none other than SCHOOL.

School is something which remains to your heart forever no matter where you live. It always had that special place within you.

School is no less than the soul of the stages you came across later in your life.

You spend your most beautiful time of life there only. You come across almost all the emotions humans have while you are in school. You feel happy when teacher praises you infront of the whole class. You know the feeling of enjoyment when suddenly you get to know that it's your games period. You feel out of the world when you score highest in the class. You felt angry when you had an argument with your friend. You came across the feeling of bonding when your friend supports you and also got to know that how bad it feels when you say goodbye to your friends cum family in the farewell with the promise of meeting at least once in a year, which you know never gonna happen.

Not just the emotions but you say 'hi' to some life lessons in school itself but realizes it later in life.

The one I learnt is Confident While Doing Wrong is Always Harmful. It was 2006 when we all were made to sit in class 8 with the students of 8th standard during our final examinations. We were the students of 6th standard. We had our environmental education exam. One of my classmates had brought chits so that he could cheat in exam. And those chits were not those typical hand written ones but were the cuttings of the text book in small pieces which made it look like chits. Literally his uniform was filled with the small small chits he prepared a night before with so much efforts and hardwork so

that he can easily cheat and can't be caught by teachers. And he was successful in doing so, which ultimately boast his confidence. Next day we had our computer applications exam and this time he took a step forward. With chits he had a page of the book, i.e., he tore the page of the book and kept it with those chits. During an exam, there was a question related to some 'home button' and the answer was in that page, he had inside his pocket. This time he was so over confident that he was adamant to do the cheating. He whispers to himself," cheating karta hu, maine thodi pakda jaunga." (Do the cheating, I won't be caught). He took out the page from the pocket and start copying the answer but this time the invigilator saw him from behind as she was walking around the whole class, the way they usually do in the examination hall but the invigilator caught him. The invigilator came near to his seat and asked, "kya kar rahe ho?" (What are you doing). He said, "kuch nahi" (nothing). She asked " kya tha haath mein aur shoes ke neeche kya h?"(What was in your hands and what you are hiding under your shoes?)

Actually, while teacher was coming near to his seat from the back, he fold the page abruptly and he tried to hide that page in his shoes hastily but unfortunately he could not do so properly and the shape of shoe turned visibly distinct due to which the inviligilator caught him red handed.

Firstly, he got a extremely tight slap from the teacher which made other students to turn around their heads. But still he was lucky enough to save himself from a severe punishment because only a page was found while checking and not the chits. So, the question is "chits kha gayi! Chits to mili nhi checking ke time." (Where are the chits disappeared because no chits were found during checking!)

So, the answer is, after getting a tight slap, teacher went to call the higher authorities for further judgement and the class has no teacher for a short span of time. Cherry on the cake was, his alloted seat in the class was the window seat and on the

other side of the window it was a playground and he managed to throw all the chits on the ground with the help of the senior sitting beside him and the chits were literally flying in the air on the playground. Imagine, he had such an ample amount of chits with him.

Till the time higher authorities came, he managed to save himself from getting severe punishment from the principal. His mother was called. As a punishment his exam paper was not accepted and was rejected or cancelled and since only the page was found, he was left with the warning.

But it is said, God always has some other plans to teach him a good lesson which he deserves because he was not at all embarrassed with what he has done. According to him it was the act of Khatron ke Khiladi and there was nothing wrong in it.

His deed reached his home as well as to all the relatives and known ones before he reached his home. As the teacher who slapped him was found out to be one of the relatives to a boy's family and she has circulated the information of his deed like a fire in the forest to everyone. Also, he was taking home tution with his cousins at his masi's place. So, the tutor also got to know about what he did.

He was made to feel embarrassed, he was humiliated by the relatives, was made fun off by the cousins. And this was not for just one or two days but he was taunted or say insulted for his deed every time they meet him.

The incidence which made him think about his deed was, it was a festival of colours 'holi' and all the relatives and cousins gathered there. He also went to his taiji's place to wish them 'happy holi.' There one of his elder cousin sisters came near to him, she kind of wrapped her arms around his shoulders from the back with extreme sweetness or should say dramatically. It was done usually when someone holds you while taunting you. It was that same situation. Then she said sarcastically, "aur kya kar rahe the!, kya kiya tumne!" (What were you

doing! What had you done!) He thought that no one knows about what he had done at least here but he was proved wrong. Everyone there also knew about his deed.
It is when he realized that what he had done just out of fun or daring had backfired him only and has destroyed his whole image of being a good child. His one small step made people to pass judgements about his conduct, behavior and also manners.
In real life also, people won't be remembering how good you are as a human but will always find a fault in you in order to judge you.
No matter it's a small deed or big deed, if you have done wrong, it will come back to you in some or other ways. And no matter how much days, months or years pass. There will always be someone who will be remembering your deed and will leave no stone upturned to remind you of your past happenings may be intentionally or unintentionally. And you have to face the repercussion every time you visit and experience your past.
Whether it's school or outside world, whether it's small as a pearl or huge as a mountain, whether it's out of dare or out of dodge, you will always have to pay back of your wrong doings and it harms no one but only You

Flairs and Glairs, a platform by a student for the students. We are esteemed youth struggling to carve out our path for our future and we follow a basic mindset Since everyone is not born with all-round skills. Joining hands with people who are born to execute it with perfection is the best way to evolve. Self-Evolution is the need of the hour but, evolving as a community is what we strive for. The initiative as kickstarted by, Founder- Mr. Shubham Shah with the motive to utilize the skillset and talent of writing has now a team of 10+ people who are actively participating into newer forms of learning and discovering talents among youngsters. We Provide platform and services like Publishing opportunities, Open mics, Workshops, Hands-on training. Operating with Brand Name of Flairs and Glairs (Publication House), we offer the chance of elevating a passionate writer to an esteemed author With Brand name Teekhe Zasbaaat. We bring to you an opportunity to get accustomed with the Public Speaking and Presenting of Thoughts along with regular challenges to brush up your inking spirit. The newest initiative to extend our services we introduced in a new writing Platform- The Glittering Fables and Ink Over Tears.

We Choose to Fly Like A Falcon than to be

a Leg Pulling Crab.

---

www.ingramcontent.com/pod-product-compliance
Ingram Content Group UK Ltd.
Pitfield, Milton Keynes, MK11 3LW, UK
UKHW022003190726
13853UKWH00004B/1711